VELVET SHIPWRECKS:

Collected Stories

Tim Wenzell

STEPHEN F. AUSTIN STATE UNIVERSITY PRESS

Production Manager: Kimberly Verhines

Cover Art: "Shipwreck" by Joseph Vernet (1714-1789) Hermitage Museum.

IBSN: 978-1-62288-915-0

For more information:
Stephen F. Austin State University Press
P.O. Box 13007 SFA Station
Nacogdoches, Texas 75962
sfapress@sfasu.edu
www.sfasu.edu/sfapress
936-468-1078

Distributed by Texas A&M University Press Consortium
www.tamupress.com

ACKNOWLEDGMENTS

"The Low Setting" previously published in *Potomac Review*. Spring 1996: 42-44.

"Downstream" previously published in *Potomac Review*. Winter 1996: 46-47.

"Surrender" previously published in *Wilderness House Literary Review*. Volume 13, No. 3, 2018.

"Ned, Steven" previously published in *Battery Pack* (a project of Neon Books). Volume III, 2018.

"The Above" previously published in *Aethlon: The Journal of Sport Literature*. XVII: 1. Fall 1999: 129-136.

"The Closet Box" previously published in *Arkansas Review*. Volume 28, Number 2, 1997: 4-11 and as Chapter 1 of the novel *Absent Children* (Writer's Digest Press, 2000).

"Ground Work" previously published in *Eclectica Magazine*. Volume 4, Number 3. Jul/Aug 2000 and *Eclectica Magazine: Best Fiction*. Racine, Wisconsin: Eclectica Press International, 2003: 280-284.

"Joey's Head" previously published in *The Oddville Press*. Summer 2018.

"Idiot Boy" previously published in *Slow Trains Literary Journal*. Volume 2, Issue 2, 2002.

"Midge" previously published in *Inertia Magazine*. Volume 2, Issue 4. October 2002

"Secret Stitches" previously published in *The Fairfield Review*, August 2003.

"Velvet Shipwrecks" previously published in *Timber Creek Review*. Volume 5, Number 3. January 1999: 63-78.

"Only Loss" previously published in Aethlon: The Journal of Sport Literature. XXXVII: 1, Fall 2019/Winter 2020: 69-73. Print.

"Bubbles" previously published in *Kaleidoscope*. Summer/Fall 2006. Number 53: 55-57.

"Slice" previously published in *Edify Fiction*, January 2019.

For more information:
Stephen F. Austin State University Press
P.O. Box 13007 SFA Station
Nacogdoches, Texas 75962
sfapress@sfasu.edu
www.sfasu.edu/sfapress

ISBN: 978-1-62288-915-0

Publishing Manager: Kimberly Verhines
Book design: Jerri Bourrous
Distributed by Texas A&M Consortium
www.tamupress.com

CONTENTS

For Bruce, who was my number one fan

CHECK POINT

WHEN THE WATERLOO Police Department stationed the sobriety check point outside of the wine-tasting festival, there was uproar. They brought in two extra officers and cleared a space on the shoulder so they could draw the chalk lines and command the wine-drinkers to walk between them. Shouts of protest marked the exit and soon word got back into the festival that they were in a trap, so everyone cut back on the wine samples and hope for the best. The Waterloo police were on this mission because, at the wine-tasting last year, a divorcing father of four hit a utility pole and put out the power all along Wellsley for over a week, forcing the police commissioner and his family to hole up in crappy Lee's Motel. Not this year, he affirmed. Get out there and make sure it doesn't happen this year.

Officer Dick Stone (a.k.a. "Richard Rock" at the station), a friend of the commissioner, was given permission to conduct sobriety tests in his own way. Instead of the usual Breathalyzer or backward ABC's or walking the line of chalk, Stone dropped change on the ground and had the unlucky drunks try to pick up the dime. A more confident stranger, perhaps from another state, tipsy and mouth-stained by cabernet from every one of the local vineyards, challenged the officer, asking whether he wanted the 1998 or the 2001 dime as he wobbled and squinted downward to the dirt, finally picking up the 1998 but falling in the process. He was arrested, dime still between his fingers, with seventeen other patrons that day.

Most notable among the arrests was the entire Wolrath family, including the driver, Fred Wolrath, who hadn't had a drink, his wife, who clearly had, and their two children. The drunk son Stevie, who had just turned sixteen and who was fed sips of wine in the middle of the fair grounds for four hours by his mother because he was antsy, insisted on saying something, fueled no doubt by the fevered hostility of the patrons still inside (searching now for sobriety) and by his mother's insistence that they all complain. The father passed the dime test from Stone, but before he could return to the car, his wife Naomi was sticking her nail into Stone's chest. It was the chardonnay talking and she always got like this, jabbing fingers into men's chests, when the chardonnay talked. Even though she was not driving, Stone arrested her for simple assault and put her in the back. Stevie followed with a rant about pigs and scum and eliminate police from the planet. He had heard 'pig' over and over during his fathers' stories of 1970's trouble, in his long-hair-big-belt-buckle-and-bell-bottoms days, before his father finally decided to comply with the law and after those days were no longer cool. Stevie didn't go into the back of the police car without a fight, however, so Stone needed the help of Saunders and McGee to get him there. Stevie had shot up two inches over the summer, and in his taller condition, even sloshed off wine samples, he thought he could handle Stone. Stevie was over-confident because he almost had the strength of an adult now, and Officer Stone looked manageable from behind Stevie's veil of alcohol.

Naomi Wolrath, from the open window, directed her daughter Annie, barely ten, to kick Stone in the shin after he had shut the door on Stevie. Without a thought Annie complied, and then Stone had no choice, hobbling in pain from what turned out to be a very sharp jab that would leave a mark, but to put Annie into the back as well in order to sort things out at the station.

Meanwhile, the sober Fred stood alone among the coins, his family locked away in a police car, and he didn't know what to do. Seven years before, he had severely injured a woman because he had driven home drunk off too many Tequilas at O'Shea's and plowed into her while she retrieved her mail in the dark— barely two weeks after he was cited for driving the car off the road and into the muddy fields of an industrial park and where he had to get his car towed out of the mire. After jail, therapy, quitting the alcohol, and community service, Fred had to keep his nose clean: not even a parking ticket or he would need to ride the bus for the rest of his life. But his family was cuffed in the back of a squad car now, and he was afraid to say anything to Stone, who clearly wanted to haul him in, too, even for a minor infraction. No one was going to put the electric out on Stone's commissioner anymore.

Fred didn't think long before he acted. He departed the coins, went to the entrance of the festival, stripped naked like he did in the days of his 70's streaking, and took off, penis flopping, across the fairgrounds, creating in the process a wave of audible and inebriated gasps. It took the efforts of Stone, Saunders, and McGee to chase, catch, and arrest him, and it took them over an hour because naked, bare-footed Fred managed to get to the stream and follow it up a good half-mile into the woods and up two steep, muddy embankments. While his family stayed locked in the back of the police car during the chase, all of the other patrons at the wine-tasting festival were able to get into their cars and leave. By the time they brought Fred down the hills and through the woods to the police cars, the fairgrounds, with the exception of the vendors, were entirely empty. The wine-tasters had escaped arrest.

Later, after the Wolraths were released from the police station, Fred told his now-sober wife that having to ride the bus every day would not be so bad after all. "I am a hero to the wine-drinkers," he proclaimed. "And now, I can get some office work done on the bus before I even get there."

DOWNSTREAM

WHEN THE BULLET finally came to a stop somewhere in his brain, everything my brother Billy was thinking ended right there in the lot, right in the middle of a thought. The six-pack dropped out of his hand onto the cement, and one of them broke off and rolled under a car. The man in the stained shirt ran with his gun past the lights, up the grass hill to the interstate, and there were just a bunch of tracks in the mud that said the stained-shirted man wore a work boot with a steel toe, the kind that millions of people get at Woolworth's. The cops that walked around the hill rubbed their chins and asked me questions and whispered 'chances were slim' of finding the guy that did Billy in.

Billy had a quick and teary funeral, and the doctors worked all night to patch his head up so they could keep the coffin open and let everybody look at him dead, so everybody could remember what he looked like alive. Mom hung around the front of the church sobbing into the undertakers Kleenexes, looking more up at Jesus on his cross than at Billy in his coffin. She was asking the statue "why" when I got up there next to her, and I looked down on Billy and he looked so calm, like sleep. His closed eyes reminded me of the mornings on Lake George when the fog rolled in, when we'd both wait on logs with our B-B guns for the water snakes to come out.

And then his dead face reminded me of an opposite, of a time when the fear was in him, on that day we stood on the ice down by the girders, and the little piece of ice Billy had walked out on broke off all of a sudden and sent him floating out to the middle of the cold creek. Billy knew if he jumped off he'd go up past his new winter coat and he'd have to wade real quick against the cold current to get back and that Mom wasn't going to take too kindly to him all wet and frozen in the fuzzy coat she'd just spent the savings on. So Billy just stood on that little iceberg as it floated out past the slanted elms. I kept thinking we'd never been that far downstream before and now there goes Billy headed into the current.

Billy balanced himself on his ice island as it twirled away, screaming 'help me Eddie' as if I were going to go splashing in to pull him ashore. I never saw Billy with a fear like that, rounding a bend he never rounded before. And now his dead hands were folded neat on his communion suit, and all of of that fear was wiped off his face, like fear was just some dirt. He wasn't going to have to worry about stepping on thin ice anymore. There's nothing like that where he's going.

Aunt Bernice and her new husband flew in from their farm and hung their heads the whole time just like everybody, and everybody took turns crying as they went up, grabbing each other by the fingers and kneeling on the little pad before the altar to wish Billy's soul well. Mom didn't let up on the crying, even at the back of the church and even after we'd left the church and closed the car doors. She'd taken a wad of Kleenex from the wooden box marked Undertaker and dirtied every tissue with tears and snot and mascara. I saw one of Dad's eyes in the rear-view mirror, red and swollen like I'd never seen an eye. He was squeezing the wheel like he wanted to twist it up on the dusty ride back, and he wasn't using the blinkers.

It was late when all the well-wishers headed home. The street was dark because all the neighbors had turned off their porch lights and their televisions. I shut the door to my room and laid down on the quilt and noticed how suddenly dark it got, so dark that I couldn't see any of myself, like I wasn't there, or I was somewhere else. I could only hear the cicadas buzzing outside the screens and it sounded like they all crawled into the room across the carpet and surrounded my bed, reminding me of Billy and all those summers when we talked about death. We promised each other whoever died first would come back in spirit and tell the other what it was like on the other side. Billy bet I was going to go first, the way I took my mini-bike up the bluff.

I'm waiting and I know he's coming. When Billy comes swooping down any night now, all the cicadas will stop. Animals get like that when the other side reaches through, even the insects, especially the insects. And in all that quiet, Billy will come riding in on some ghost-iceberg through the screen. He'll still be going around that bend in the creek, except now the fear will be wiped off his face, like fear was just some dirt. Billy will tell me his streams aren't so cold anymore and there are no more fuzzy coats and people worrying about getting them wet. Billy's streams take him wherever he wants to go, and he'll come riding back to keep his promise to me. He'll tell me his body is all gone, about giant flowers that grow high into the sky and about the breeze that chills you and warms you at the same time. You don't have to stay on the ground if you don't want because you don't have a body to keep you there, he'll tell me, just like all those summer nights we talked. Billy will want me to convince Mom and Dad that he's a happy ghost.

I can tell he's coming. I feel a little breeze blowing through the screen, some air coming out from the other side. The cicadas aren't so loud anymore, and pretty soon they'll stop altogether to make way for Billy to come through. I'm just going to lay here in the dark and wait it out.

THE CLOSET BOX

AFTER THE MASKED hoodlums broke in on a stiff winter night and took his little brother Benjamin from the crib, Eddie Shemanski built a confessional in the wall of his closet that fit him precisely and hid him quiet behind the hanging sweaters. He built the box out of the two by fours and the drywall scraps his father had left in the attic. Eddie would hide in the box, retreating there every time he heard a knock at the door, and sometimes when the phone rang and sometimes when he thought that his father wasn't really his father. He would look out from his breathing holes and wait for the answer at the door, wait for the reply to the phone call, wait to see his father's loafers squashing his shag carpet as he opened the closet door, calling his name and asking: "Where did you get to you little son of a bitch?"

Eddie saw a customer in the restaurant one night who looked exactly like his father. "Well, they say everyone in the world has someone that looks exactly like them," at least twenty-five employees whispered to him. The striking similarities, down to the shape of the teeth, gave Eddie the same dream night after night. He was fishing on a river in the dream, playing catch with a man sitting at a table. A candle burned in front of the man, as he sat holding his fishing pole with his crooked set of teeth.

Sometimes, early in the morning just after he awoke, or when his father walked down the hall between innings to go to the toilet, Eddie became convinced it was that same restaurant customer, and now he had barged into his house, coming to reclaim his long-lost son.

After the dreams stopped and he forgot about his father's look-alike, Eddie started smoking his mother's Kools in the closet box. He found a way to take them there four at a time along with one of her Bic lighters. He'd be careful to plug the holes and close the door tight. Once, when he left the door open, a graveyard of smoke drifted and settled on the floor of his room. He tried desperately to vent the smoke out his raised window with a pile of papers. Then he heard the squeak of the floorboards in the hallway and his mother's voice calling for laundry. Set the lighter on low, Eddie told himself as he entered his chamber. He remembered the accident with the tall flame and the top of his box and the severe burns that encrusted the palms of his hands with blisters. He had told his parents that the blisters came from a coffee pot at the Scout outing.

Eddie stashed an empty tuna can in the far corner of the box. He enclosed it behind a cardboard flap, and his butts filled it up each week. He'd slide the stuffed Starkist can into his trousers and take it down two flights to the kitchen on trash night and quickly empty it beneath wads of wet paper towel or coffee grounds or shaved apple slices from another one of his mother's charred pies. Sometimes a butt or two would lodge in his underwear and make his crotch smell like tobacco. Sometimes, they slid down a trouser leg and fell to the floor. Eddie would flash his fingers to the floor and grab the stray butts before his father looked up from the box scores.

"Eddie's clothes...they smell like ciggies, honey. They smell like ciggies, lots of them," he heard his mother say to his father from their bed one night. She had just come up from the basement, and Eddie closed his windows and the sound of the crickets off and rested his ear lightly upon the air vent as their voices echoed up.

"I smoked on the corner of Tenth and Reed for twelve years," his father said. "Eddie knows that from all the Pete stories. He would just tell me I had no room to talk if I confronted him about it."

"At least let him know about the dangers of smoking...show him pictures of emphysema patients or something..."

"Why don't I just show myself the pictures? I have no room to talk. I smoke two packs a day, honey, and I have no room to talk."

Eddie heard the light click off as he watched the reflection die off the vent wall. He calculated that his mother smoked three packs a day.

He crawled into bed after he flicked off his own light. For almost seven hours he lay awake, and then Eddie decided he would begin to smoke nude. Eddie figured the smell could simply be washed away. "Besides," he thought, "I won't give dad the damned satisfaction."

Eddie's smoking ritual became like taking a shower from that moment on; he left his clothes in a folded pile in front of the box, then stepped in, chain-smoked four Kools, and sealed the door behind him. He usually waited until his Uncle Pete came over to light up, waiting for the moment of the knock and for his uncle's voice to trail off down the walk. Then he'd sneak into his parent's room during the commotion at the door, putting his hands into the pockets of his mother's windbreaker, rummaging the pack that was always there. He would unzip his fly and fill it with stolen cigarettes, five or six of them. (When he would get greedy and go for seven or eight, he would always manage to tear up a cigarette in the teeth of his zipper and leave a trail of tobacco leaves). Each night, the time of his thefts came just before seven-thirty, when baseball was coming on, the event his father lived for. Baseball: Eddie's recurring hell, coming out of the television six nights a week.

Eddie hated summer. He hated the heat and the humidity, and he hated the insects. He despised the noisy ones, crickets and cicadas and such, anything that gathered together and kept him up and worrying about bugs crawling into the room. But mostly, Eddie hated baseball. When his Uncle Pete would come over with his Baseball Encyclopedia, he knew all the ear plugs in the world wouldn't shut out the trivia questions booming back and forth across the living room between his father and his uncle, deep into the night. McCovey, Ruth, Maris, Gehrig, Greenberg, Campanis, Fingers, Robinson, Frisch and Williams; the names tumbled on and on, one after the other. Only, league, consecutive, and most. Years and careers, games and hits, losses and wins. The words merged and echoed in foreign syntax, down the hall and beneath Eddie's door, leaking through the pillows he had mashed in failure against his ears. "Give me something I haven't heard," they dared each other, vibrating the drywall. "Give me something I haven't heard."

II

EDDIE BROUGHT IN a boom-box for one of his dishwashing shifts at the restaurant, after the drunk cook had dropped his radio into the gravy. He brought it in because Lou the manager had said, "No more radios behind the line," and for the drunk cook to get himself together or else. Lou pointed out that Eddie was perfectly free to put something on the plate shelf, and he made a little space for him next to the foil. Eddie brought the boom-box in to soothe his night with some reggae. He brought it in to show up the night cooks.

"Put the game on," the drunken cook demanded. "Let us hear the game." Eddie looked up at the clock, and it read seven-thirty.

"I hate baseball, it's my radio, fuck you," Eddie replied as he sprayed down a rack of soup bowls.

The nice cook approached him around nine o'clock and asked if he could simply get a score, with the promise that he would put Marley immediately back on.

"Sure, but only if you make it quick," Eddie said.

The nice cook cranked the dial with his wet hand and then stood in Eddie's way and listened to the buzz injected through Eddie's boom box by the dish machine. The announcer fought through the buzz and called a ball and then another ball and then a strike and then a foul, a foul, a foul, a ball, a pop-up for the second out and then three strikes in a row for the third out. "We go to the top of the seventh," the announcer said out of the rinse-cycle static, "with the score Reds eleven, Phils one."

The nice cook gave a groan and walked away without changing the station back, drying his hand on his apron, his gait slow and hunched.

"Something wrong?" Eddie asked. "Eleven to one...is that bad?

The nice cook looked back, puzzled like a mathematician with a piece of chalk. "Bad?" he replied. "Bad?"

Eddie pulled a hot rack out of the other end of the machine, slipping the plates quickly into a stack with the tips of his fingers.

"Dude, they're down by ten runs," the nice cook said. "Whadya mean, bad...that's as bad as it gets."

"Well, how many points is a run?" Eddie asked at the shelf, not caring for runs or points or anything at all to do with baseball (uncles or fathers).

The nice cook straightened up, widened his eyes in disbelief and retied his apron strings by the sink. "A run is a run, there's no points in baseball."

"You mean you don't get any extra points for sliding in fancy or anything?" Eddie asked.

"Where in the hell did you grow up?" came the voice of the drunk cook. "What are you, some kind of sports idiot?" He held aloft a New York strip, smoking and well-done on its way to a platter. "Didn't you ever play baseball?"

Eddie didn't answer. He only switched back his station and turned the volume up, as the reverberating cadence of a reggae song divided him into his solitude. The drunken cook began to laugh, and the nice cook chuckled his way back into his fold. "Unbelievable," he heard them say to each other, as they reached together and pulled off a bundle of tickets from the wheel. "Unfucking believable."

Eddie never told the cooks or the waiters or Benny the week-night dishwasher of his confessional, of his peculiar habit of retreating there. He didn't tell them what he did when he went home, how he closed the door to his room, locking it and listening. He didn't tell them about his journey through a forest of hanging sweaters to smoke his cigarettes. He never told them about his private little problem.

Never in his darkness did Eddie bother long enough to think: "Why don't I just sit on my radiator and blow it out my window? Crawl out on the roof? Walk out to the woods, sit down on a log, and smoke it in one of the clearings?" Eddie smoked mostly because he was angry at the prospect of another long night of baseball and the loud slurring of drunken trivia and the clinking of empty beer bottles on their way to the recycling tub. The dark interior of that box would embrace him. The glow of the cigarette that lingered there between the walls would mesmerize him. The walls muffled away the outside world like the encroaching air of a coffin. Eddie sealed himself in a stagnant little universe, comfortably trapped, comfortably alive and alone. "I love to take big drags in here," Eddie thought. "I like to blow them away invisible." But he also smoked because he was nervous, and that was why he went to his closet box, because he was nervous.

III

EDDIE'S MOTHER ANSWERED the door one night and found no one there. He heard her from the box as she opened the door, guessing she was peering about the bushes, hearing the click as she flicked on the porch light. Then she screamed, and Eddie's heart grew rapid as he listened for the sound of a stranger's footsteps on the stairs. He anticipated the planned trip unfolding into his bedroom to steal him away with scarves and blindfolds. (His mother had jumped back at a Luna moth that had crashed into the screen, though there was no way Eddie, in his darkness, could know this). Eddie listened as she went sobbing from the front door to the bedroom in hurried steps. His father sighed deeply and got up from his game. Feeling safety, Eddie slid out of the wall and over to the vent. His mother began talking, in waves of wails, about Benjamin.

"It's been well over two years," she said. "They never found the men and I can't help thinking what they've done to our little baby or where he might be. I can't help thinking they planned it all out, and if we could have seen behind those masks, we might know who they were."

She sobbed for a while. It came up the vent and Eddie lay down on his shag carpet and looked up at the stained ceiling, waiting for her to stop. He heard the cheering coming out of the television in the other room. His father was missing something exciting, maybe a home run or a double-play grounder, maybe a bench-clearing brawl.

"Remember how they came in, Harry?" she sobbed with more control. "Remember how they put us face-down on the floor at gunpoint and marched right up the stairs and into his room?"

"Yes, honey, we've been over it. Remember what the counselor said, we should try to put it behind..."

"I'm screaming at moths, for Christ's sake," she said. "Two and a half years later and I'm jumping at bugs on the screen."

"I'll bet that O'Hara kid is up to his knocking pranks again," his father said. "Damned son of a bitch kids have no regard, no regard."

"The detective couldn't find a motive. I can't believe there was no motive," she continued in her sob state. "Someone was spying on us and knew where to go. They wanted Benjamin, somebody wanted Benjamin in the top room. They came in and stole him like he was a television or a VCR or an expensive necklace."

His father gave a sigh that hissed up the vent. Eddie figured he wanted to get back to his chair in the living room because somebody was mounting a rally.

"There's nothing left we can do, honey, you know that," his father said. "What's the point any more?"

Eddie's mother sobbed long and low and his ear hurt from resting it on the louvers of the vent plate. So he got up and went down into the kitchen to survey the garbage situation. His father came walking out from the bedroom, a brisk walk past the kitchen door, pulled like a magnet to the cheers coming out of the living room television. Baseball: he clapped his hands three times and hollered "Yeah!"

Eddie watched him as he stood next to his chair when the score came up and as a commercial flashed on and then as he finished his backwash. Eddie looked over to the corner of the kitchen: his father had already taken out the garbage. Dammit—he would need to find another way to get rid of the butts in his tuna can. He considered smuggling them out in his underwear on his way to the restaurant. Instead, he stuffed them in an old sock, one of the ones with the holes and the permanent sweat stains off the survival weekend. He dropped the sock between the beams of the wall, figuring he would be fully grown, and his parents long gone by the time it was finally unearthed.

IV

EDDIE BOUGHT SOME joints from Benny the weeknight dishwasher one afternoon in the lot, just after Lou the manager left for the liquor order. He had smoked some pot at the Lenape Valley Jamboree with some of the Life Scouts that spring, and, upon getting stoned, he had liked the way the fire leaped to the lighter fluid. He had watched the trees flashing in and out of his sight and he had liked the way the black leaves moved, like quivering jellyfish...and he had liked the way the eyes of the scouts wrapped in a circle around the flames, dark socket to dark socket, connected. So he said "yes" when Benny asked him if he got high, and then he bought some joints from him out of the ounce Benny pulled from his duffel bag. Eddie unzipped his fly, slid them in, and zipped slowly back up, a notch at a time.

"What are you doing?" Benny asked him. "They have these things now called pockets."

"Yeah, but you don't know my parents. It gets practically like a Nazi police station going home sometimes," Eddie said.

"You mean they actually search you?" Benny asked.

"Oh, no. But the way they look at me, especially back when I was snagging Mom's cigarettes from the junk drawer and putting them in my pockets, it was like they knew." Eddie patted his crotch. "I don't want to chance it. God knows what would happen if they found out I smoked a drug like this."

Eddie went home and searched for his mother's lighter in the box. He had tossed his tuna can and now there was nothing behind the cardboard flap: no butts, no can, no lighter. The lighter might have dropped down between the beams with his sock full of butts, the way his hamster Elvis had done five years back when it escaped through the hole in the aquarium. He would have to get another lighter, or maybe a couple of packs of matches. He would need another tin can, too, maybe a soup-sized one this time around.

Eddie disrobed and smoked his first joint the night of a doubleheader, the night his Uncle Pete had just come from an argument with his Aunt Rita. He listened to the scraping of his uncle's shoes on the walk before he went in (scraping shoes meant his uncle had started early on the beer-drinking, probably at Fitzgerald's Pub, and he would spend the night on the cot). Sure enough, he heard his father tell him to park his car up on the grass. "You don't want a ticket like you got the last time you stayed," he said.

"Never paid the son of a bitch, either," his uncle said. "A man should be able to park on the street." Eddie heard the hum of the refrigerator motor as it rattled the bottles. Uncle Pete was hunting for the imported beer.

"Are you ready for six hours of baseball?" his father asked. Then he heard their echoes from the kitchen, laughing mostly, talking about Aunt Rita "the bitch" and how Uncle Pete was going to take her poodle out to the woods and let it loose. The television had not yet been turned on and their voices carried up through the silent house like prayers in a church, penetrating his black universe.

"Damned thing will starve to death, too, because there'll be nobody out there to feed it filet mignon and spring water," Uncle Pete said. "And you know what I'll tell Rita...I'll tell her I tied its little paws together and laid it in the driveway and backed over the damned thing...crunch, crunch, crunch with the tires back and forth over and over until I pulverized it and I buried the pieces in sandwich bags down by the creek or something. I'll tell her that and then sit back and watch how riled up she'll get after she can't find the miserable little thing under any of the beds. I'll laugh like Jesus all the way to Fitzgerald's.

Eddie flicked the match and the flame lit up the blackness of his box, and he nervously touched it to the end of the joint. He held in the wicked smoke, held it long enough to spit it out in a quiet cough, just the way the Life Scouts had instructed him. He did it again and then he did it again and then he imagined the smoke hanging by circular wires around his chest, halos unseen. I am the planet Saturn, he thought.

V

1972. THE FIRST ball game Eddie ever went to and the first year of the new stadium. It was state-of-the art because you were never going to need grass again. "Astro-Turf is the greatest invention ever conceived in the history of man," his father told him, patting Eddie on his wet hair and directing him to the station wagon. "No more lousy-paid gardeners planting, reaping, growing, cutting, growing, cutting, growing, cutting, growing, cutting." He backed down the driveway, stopped, looked out at the crabgrass. "Wish I could afford the stuff for our yard, what with the way the mower's been acting."

Eddie sat in the yellow seats of the big new stadium holding a tub of Coke, between his father and William. William, his older brother, had just given up a guinea-pig breeding business and started selling cancer insurance to stricken families. William would get customers names from the hospitals and knock on their doors and get himself inside to open his brief case and talk payment plans. Sometimes he'd hang out at The Cemetery Stop and interrupt people while they were headstone-shopping, throwing out a line or two of condolences. Then, he'd rattle off his memorized speech, the one that guaranteed a sell.

Five years back, William had left the house on a Harley headed for the Northwest Territories, the night after he'd given Eddie a pet hamster for his sixth birthday, asking only that he name it "Elvis." Eddie wondered how a guy such as his brother, at one point of his life headed for the Northwest Territories on a Harley, could come back home and peddle to grieving families. He wondered where along the line he converted himself into a money-worshiping grub and how he could put on those false faces, cemented with remorse and covering the cracks of his rotting greed.

His father was explaining the significance of the third-base coach bringing out the line-up card to the umpires, talking over Eddie and his tub of soda to William. William wanted, in his wiser state, to learn more about a game he never had an interest in as a child. William had grown closer to his father since he'd moved back. He'd taken his old room on the bottom floor and had his long hair cut off. But he had grown closer mostly because he had brought home a load of money and helped his father out with mortgage payments and bought a new set of sliding doors and ratchet sets and such.

"You see, the Phils have been on a long losing streak, eleven in a row now," his father said. "Eventually, after you can't find any good excuses for losing any more, you begin to think it's bad luck that's nailed your whole team. You get superstitious, you try to do things differently. Now, look down and see what we have going on at home plate...a manager telling his third base coach to go out to the mound instead of himself. Maybe we'll win if I send someone else out, he's thinking. Maybe I'm bad luck, maybe some witch doctor put a curse on me. I've got to do something now, in a hurry, before it's too late. Before they decide to fire my ass."

Eddie only remembered their voices suspended above him, like a high wire just out of reach, talking about line-drive double plays and when to sacrifice and should they use the suicide squeeze, and he lost himself in the black swirl of ice cubes dancing in his Coke. They talked on and on, into the game and above the rows of voices that shot out in a recurring spasm of boos and catcalls, as the Phillies dropped fly balls and got tagged out at home and struck out, batter after batter in the dead heat. His father reached over Eddie with his scorecard and his little yellow pencil, showed William the numbers assigned to each position. Then his father sighed in irritation and finally asked Eddie to switch seats because it would be easier to explain things. Another rain of boos descended from above.

Sitting on the end, Eddie watched a program flutter down from the upper deck, the pages wing-like in its downward flight, a paper bird. Eddie looked at his father and William gathered around the numbers. He could have gotten up and lost himself in the upper deck, between the legs of ushers and vendors, and they never would have noticed. He looked at the remaining ice cubes melting at the bottom of his tub and flung the container into the air in one clean jerk. He watched in his anger as the tub sailed high above the heads of the crowd, a crowd now standing and pumping their arms furiously over a misplayed ball, anger and contortion spread like butter over their faces. His projectile caught a momentary breeze that carried it ten rows out, then turned for its rocket-ride downward, ice cubes weighing the bottom of it and dropping it like a bag of bricks, directly onto the head of an old woman. The hard edge of the cardboard sliced full force against her withered forehead, and Eddie got up and watched from the railing as it opened her up. The blood ran down over her lava-rock face, streaming across her eyes as they flickered shut. The entire row, who Eddie guessed were grandsons and sons, converged upon her in terror, calling for medical help and looking back into the crowd for the perpetrator of the vicious act. An older boy in a green jersey looked directly at him, stared up at Eddie as his father called him back to his seat. The green boy was swept away down the row in a furious melee of security people and emergency help. Eddie eyed the old woman's trembling hands as they passed on the stretcher, as they moved beneath the quieted crowd and away from the oblivious ballplayers hundreds of yards down. He watched her disappear into the tunnel, followed by her grandsons, and then her sons. His father looked up from his scorecard, wrinkled his nose, and muttered, "I wonder what happened over there."

1972. The last ball game Eddie ever attended.

VI

EDDIE GOT STONED in his box one night and thought back to that day at the game. He remembered the old lady and the hurried medical men and all the family members swallowed as a parade into the tunnel. Eddie feared that the old lady had died, maybe on her way to the emergency room. They had bandaged her up and sewn her old skin together during the bumpy ambulance ride, but the shock of the blow had seized her heart and didn't let go until it had stopped beating. Maybe she was the nicest woman on her block, with flower boxes and cats and home-made biscuits. Her sons and grandsons adored her and took her to ball games and listened to her talk about the old-timers, Babe Ruth and Jimmie Foxx and Rogers Hornsby. She would tell them about the ticker-tape parades for the A's down Broad Street on chilly October weekdays. But now the sons and grandsons were left with only an obituary reading 'Very Remarkable Lady' after Eddie's pointless act. They were left in a somber waiting room to question the absurdity of her stadium death. Angry, crying, bewildered, the sons raised their voices into shouts down empty hallways, vowing that whoever did this to their mother would be hunted down.

The boy in the green jersey: the look on his face returned, it came out of the brilliant sun of that afternoon game and entered into Eddie's sealed chamber. That boy must have seen him throw his empty tub into the air, he must have looked closely at him and remembered where he was sitting, and then had gone and blurted it out in the waiting room. "It was a kid that did it, a little kid. I saw him throw the thing into the air, Pop. I saw him come over to the railing and watch grandmother bleeding. I'd recognize the kid anywhere. He thought the whole thing was funny."

A sudden revelation seized Eddie and pulled him down to a seated position in his box, constricted him as he snuffed his roach against the wall. Green jersey, green jersey, green jersey: one of the men who abducted Benjamin had worn a green jersey, a green jersey with white numbers, the number sixteen (he recalled the testimony of his wailing mother). Eddie tried to remember if that was the number on the boy, because it was the number on the man, the man who had made his parents lie face-down on the rug. Yes, he pictured the day seven years back, the crowd rising to its feet and scrambling down the row to help to the fallen woman. The boy, he remembered, the boy stood up on his seat, stood and glared back at Eddie with those furry eyebrows, that hairy anger. No doubt remained: the boy had seen him throw his empty soda. He had witnessed his grandmother's executioner with one long and unforgettable stare. The number sixteen was there, spread across his chest; there was no other number. Eddie looked into the blackness: sixteen.

But it couldn't be, it wasn't possible. How could the boy track him down, a little boy's face in a crowd a level up? Why would he wait to seek his vengeance, five years after the fact? The boy was in his twenties by now, bigger than his jersey with a furry moustache to match his furry eyebrows and driving a used car, out on dates and beer-drinking binges past his curfew, no doubt. Surely, he forgot, maybe during the summer when he shot up two inches, the summer he grew out of his green jersey. *No. There was no way. It was ludicrous to even think it.* It couldn't have been the same person.

The television was blaring downstairs now and someone was fouling off pitch after pitch. Uncle Pete was asking a question in the foreign syntax of his baseball trivia, slurring it out loud across the room. "Who was the only guy to hit for the cycle in each league?" he asked. It was only the television for a while and Eddie figured his dad was done in, that the Petester had him down another beer. He heard it go to commercial, and then, in the middle of a lingo, the name "Bob Watson" came out of his father's throat, from out of the easy chair and across the carpet. His loud and certain answer caused Eddie's uncle to rattle the television tray with an "almost had you, you son of a bitch." Bob Watson...what a simple, idiotic name, Eddie thought. This guy does one freak-of-nature thing in one miserable career and lives forever in baseball trivia, hailed by drunken losers.

He listened as his father and uncle got silent for a time, when he could hear only the game, the faint echo of a sparse crowd clapping, the steady drone of the man's voice as the pitches came in. Nice, really, Eddie thought. A soothing, pleasant sound, like a sprinkle of warm water running over you.

In Eddie's black little universe, baseball was an echo, always trying to reach in and grab hold of him, always trying to rattle him. Now, he would try to like it. He focused on his father's voice, his uncle's replies. "Ball three...if Hobose gets aboard, it's a sure steal," his father said. "The guy's only been caught once all year." Eddie wished the guy aboard, and he wished him nailed at second base.

Eddie wanted to wrap the foreign syntax around him, embrace it, like it. After all, William had done it, and whenever he called from Washington, he and his father spent the first five minutes on the phone, talking about his Congressional pursuits and then the next two hours talking baseball (William was involved in a campaign to bring back the Senators). If Eddie learned to like baseball like his brother, he could sit down on the couch and watch the game, ask some tough trivia, make their beer runs. He would just need to come down the steps from his room and ask his Uncle Pete to slide over.

Eddie tried; he squeezed his temple and pretended to like baseball, but it didn't matter. Darkness, noise, closed eyes: they couldn't keep out the number sixteen, and that peculiar, dying-grass color of the boy's jersey. Eddie broke his link to the voices downstairs, to the drone of the game, surrendered to the thought gnawing at the edges of his closet box: "I killed a lady."

VII

EDDIE LAID HIS head against the beam, tired from the long day. He had gotten up at four in the morning after a car alarm had gone off down on Catherine

Street, and he could not return to sleep because the cut on his thumb had begun to throb. He had gone downstairs to wash it in the bathroom sink, and his father had clicked on the hall light to ask if everything was all right.

"Some plates slipped during a bus pan slam and I tried to catch them before they hit the floor and one of the broken pieces got me...Lou the manager wrapped my cut in band-aids and told me it was too busy to go get stitches," Eddie had told him. Eddie had stayed on and worked late and didn't think about the rinsed sauces and the beet juice and the lamb scraps and whatnot running down the dirty china and getting down inside his band-aids, settling into his cut. His father had warned him over the running water that if the throbbing persisted, they should both head to the doctor when he awoke. But Eddie never slept, and now here he was, in his box with the pain returning to his thumb, with the day now gone deep into the night, without a word to his father. The droning of the baseball game injected him like a sedative, and he rested the point of his skull against the corner of the box and fell asleep there.

When Eddie awoke, the game had been clicked off. His father and mother had gone to bed, and his uncle had fallen dead asleep on the cot, leaving only the muffled crickets chirping outside his box. Eddie didn't know where he was during the first few seconds out of sleep; blackness brought no familiar things to place him into the conscious world, so he hovered in transition like a bird on a storm front. His mind worked, trying to grasp any tangible thing so that it could tell Eddie any bit of information. Images came and went, slides on the wall, shadows rising tall from all sides, monolithic overcoats approaching and converging; bars, shadows of bars, left and right, tapering below his feet. A crib, he was in a crib, long and narrow, bars rising beyond arm's length, the shadows of other things above him, the swaying of the tree branches hitting the house, the long and evil fingers of strangers coming out of overcoats, reaching down. "I'm in a crib... I'm in a crib, a crib, who am I?" he silently questioned the unfolding blackness. "Where did I wake up?"

Eddie leaped out at the vast nothingness, thrashed at the imaginary forms swelling and disintegrating before him. He felt out into the blackness. "Solid wall, solid wall...the ceiling, I can touch the ceiling" he thought. "Wait, no crib, I'm not in a crib, there are no overcoats or dead branches or mobiles hanging and twisting on their strings, no faces coming closer. I'm in a box, my closet box, the one that I built with the two by fours and the drywall scraps out of the attic, the place no one knows about." He felt his nakedness, and then his hand felt along the floor for the roach he remembered snubbing. "I should find out what time it is," he thought as he inhaled the remaining hit.

It was five-thirty in the morning when Eddie came out of his box. He lay on top of his sheets, fully awake, and watched the light coming back to the yard. His bed: now he remembered the night they came, just about this time, two and a half years back, the night he awoke and heard the pleas from the den, the whimpering of his mother, his father's offer, "Take what you want but please leave us be."

And then the reply, "Face down dammit." That was all he remembered them saying, "Face down dammit." They came up the stairs, two or three steps at a time, boot to boot... Eddie remembered smelling strangers in the house, watching shadows coming across the light cracks from the hallway, feeling the draft of the winter night rushing into his room. He slid under the bed and curled up beneath the balled-up quilt, closed his eyes, tried to shut things out, pretend there was no world out there, no sound of strange footsteps or a crying baby or the screaming pleads as the front door slammed shut, Benjamin stolen.

Eddie wasn't quite sure, but in the muffled cocoon of his quilt, he thought he remembered the men stopping in front of his room, talking in precise whispers. "Eddie...where is he...he's not in his room...he's sleeping over at a friend's, probably the Helmuth kid...dammit now what...." Then the men went and took the baby in the next room, in plan B of their quickening moments. Eddie was sure, as he replayed the events in his mind, sure as he'd ever been of anything: the men had come for him, not Benjamin. After all, Benjamin had done nothing to harm anyone, save an extra-dirty diaper. Neither had his mother or father, save cutting someone off on 676. "I, on the other hand, have killed a woman," Eddie thought. "I nailed her in the head with an empty cup and her family has come to hunt me down."

His green-jerseyed man had now assumed full imaginative reality: scruffy, mustached, tattoos of ships up the arms, vengeance-motivated. He was waiting somewhere nearby, in a turned-off van, for Eddie to put out his light and fall to sleep. He was getting his ski mask ready, and he was going to slip in any night now and abduct him, tie him up and put him into the back of his van, overpower little Eddie with his battle-shipped forearms. Too frightening: Eddie started sleeping nights nude in his closet box. With two long nails, Eddie hammered one of his pillows to a wall of his box, marking the place where he would rest the back of his skull and doze off.

VIII

"PLEASE, OFFICER, DO what you can," came his mother's wails from the bottom of the house, "he should have been home by now." Eddie awoke in his box, calculating where in the house the voice came from: porch, it was coming from the porch. His mother was talking to a policeman—he could see the flashing lights coming through the breathing holes. He could hear the dispatches entering the closet, out from the speakers on their dashes. His mother was worried about him, because the last she had seen him, he was in his room. "I only fell asleep during 'Jeopardy,'" she told the man over the phone. "I would have heard him go out with the way he always slams the door. And why in the world would Eddie sneak out?"

Sobbing some more and some more, she went on and Eddie listened and stayed in the box, afraid to come out but wanting to tell her he'd been inside the house the whole time. If he came out he would have to divulge his secret, tell them about his secret little place. He'd have to let them in on everything, the times after school when he sawed and drilled and screwed the closet box into the wall before they both got home from work, and the times he'd carry the hammer back through the living room under his coat to return it to the bottom of the tool box. He'd have to tell them about the panic, when he heard the knocks and the rings and how everything scared him and made him retreat between the walls. "I'm next, I know I'm the next—they're out there somewhere planning to come and get me," he would finally say, and he'd seek the comfort of his father's hairy arms, where Eddie would lose all control in a fit of unbroken tears. Between sobs, he would tell his father about the game, about the tub of melting ice cubes he sailed in anger into the air. "I killed a lady because I am jealous of William," he would finally blurt out wetfaced into his father's stomach. "And I hate everybody."

Eddie stayed in the box until the flashing lights went away, as the police cars started up and roared away towards 676. He heard his parents sobbing from their bedroom, and this time he didn't crawl to the vent to listen. Rather, he tried to close off their sobs with other thoughts. He put his thumbs inside his ears and wondered: would the new kid that Lou the manager just hired be able to handle a Saturday night slam? What if he went down in flames? Would Lou beg Eddie to to come in in the middle of the night to bail him out? Eddie figured it might be a good time to hit Lou up for a raise. A quarter? Fifty cents? A dollar? Maybe more.

After his parents went to sleep, Eddie snuck down the stairs and out the door. He walked up the road, shirt buttoned wrong, to the Buy-Rite, feeling the cool breeze revealing itself through the trees along the way. He stood under the lamp and pulled a quarter from his pocket, and he deposited it into the pay phone. 645-2109: his father answered on the first ring, sounding frightened, a crackling hello that expected some horrible news.

"Dad. it's me Eddie."

"Eddie, Oh my God, Eddie. Where are you, what happened?"

"A long story, dad, a long story. I was running away. I was scared and I was running away. But I'm all right now and I'm coming home, if you promise not to ask any questions."

"Where are you?"

"I'll be home soon, in the morning," Eddie said. He hung up the phone, sat down on the curb beneath the lamp and buttoned his shirt the right way. Eddie looked out at the road as it continued past the last street- lamps, and he thought briefly about running away. Then he looked down to the gravel all around his shoes and he wondered whether the Phillies had won.

GROUND WORK

DADDY SENT ME to my room for kicking Shakespeare's water bowl across the kitchen floor and yelling that it was a stupid place to feed the dog. I was marching up the stairs when I heard Mommy telling Daddy how I spit on the couch in the afternoon, but I really didn't spit the way she was telling. It was just a little drool that I didn't do on purpose, something that came out while I was watching a commercial. Mommy asked me if I was some kind of animal and said no wonder people sit on those plastic slipcovers, and then she told me to go practice my baton in the attic and then go to my room for the night. I'd rather be in the attic than in my room. I hate my room.

Lucky for me I still got a couple of Mommy's Tareytons on the windowsill behind the curtain. I really had to sneak those matches off the credenza good. If they ever found my coffee can of butts at the top of the closet, I don't know what they'd do. There must be five hundred butts in that can. I'd probably try to make them feel guilty and tell them it was all their fault for smoking in the first place and setting the bad example and sending me to my room where they knew I hated to go and what else could I do but take up smoking. They'd say on top of smoking it was stealing.

Sometimes I still get dizzy when I smoke. I don't know whether it's Mommy's lousy cigarettes and I just hate the taste compared to menthols, or maybe that's just the way it is with all smokers. Marta says the dizziness has nothing to do with the taste or with cigarettes at all for that matter. She says it's a sign I'm going to be bleeding soon, that she got the same spells all last summer driving around with Birddog.

Marta's going to be setting me up with a biker on Sunday night from Fergusonville. I always liked those movies of the seventies showing skinny girls in bell-bottoms leaning back on their boyfriend's sissy bars, with hair in their eyes and showing the peace sign and lighting their cigarettes like they didn't care about anything. I just hope this biker dude isn't too hairy, and I hope he doesn't smell like whisky because I might not want to kiss him.

I want to lose my virginity on Sunday.

While we were in the lavatory, I told Marta I wanted to lose my virginity, so she set me up with this guy Mort the biker. Mort talked like one of those bad guys you always see on crime shows. She told me a couple of her girlfriends lost their virginity with Mort, and they thought he was great. She said he was good at getting you to bleed. Marta told me to forget about him after the night we do it (hopefully this Sunday) and not to fall in hopeless love and get attached to him. Mort just liked to do virgins one after the other and didn't fall in love, she told me. Mort was forty.

I guess I kicked Shakespeare's bowl across the kitchen because I'm mad at everything. I'm afraid of bleeding, and I'm tired of waiting for it. I'm so tired of waiting for it that being afraid doesn't matter anymore, and I just want it to come and then go away and just be a memory that I can write about in my diary. Every time I see Marta, I think about her and Birddog, and I get jealous. There's nothing worse than Marta having something on you, especially calling herself a woman.

I keep asking myself "What is it like?" I keep wondering and imagining the whole thing: how to lay and how to spread and how I'll be able to breathe. I remember the brawl in field hockey, laying at the bottom of the pile over at Bilgate, screaming at all the girls to let me up because I couldn't breathe. I hope it's not like that. If I have to scream for Mort to let me up, he just might zip up and walk off laughing and leave me alone with my spread legs. Word might get around that I screamed in his ear, and then I'd never lose my virginity.

Marta changed after she did it. Come to think of it, so did Stacey and Rita and Libby and Maureen and Sylvia. They all changed, like some of those pods from Invasion of the Body Snatchers were put next to each of their beds while they were asleep. The pods took them over while virgins like me sat back and noticed.

Marta used to be my best friend. I was flipping through one of my old diaries the other day, and I noticed how we got together every single day the summer we were seven. There was an entry about the state fair and the stuffed pink panda she won, and an entry about a sleepover party on Betty's birthday where she threw up grape soda, and the entry about the time Marta went down to Point Pleasant with me in the back seat of the old station wagon. That was the day we saw the car go off the bridge and sink into the bay. We just kept going past the broken cement, and Daddy told us not to worry, that the family escaped and swam to the bay shore.

I know better now, of course. I'm not seven anymore, and I've seen too many shows where the car sinks into the water and everyone drowns. Birddog was telling me about air pressure and water pressure and how people panic and scream and claw and try to open the doors. Then they roll down the windows to let the water come into the car. The force of the water hits them in such a rush that they are pinned into their seats and can't ever escape. Daddy lied to us; he didn't want us thinking about death while we were on vacation. Mommy told me that when she was drunk off her whiskies.

Marta's changed now, though. I hardly see her anymore, and when I do, she's got her boyfriend all wrapped around her with his tongue in her ear. Marta had her bellybutton pierced the other day, and she plans to get a tattoo of a clipper ship on her ass. She's been cursing a lot lately, too, imitating Birddog, I guess. Marta told me on the phone this morning that Birddog got drunk last night and burned down his old tree fort with some lighter fluid.

Sometimes I don't want to go through with the whole sex thing. Sometimes I don't want to change. Sometimes I'd rather stay in my room, move the furniture and set the dining room table in my dollhouse and just pretend. Pretending is safe, and safe feels good. Barbie is still sitting in her Camaro, and I can't remember the last time I played with her.

I wish I could freeze time, take some pages out of that old diary I found from that one summer and drop some magic dust on them or something. Then I could just close my eyes and open them to little Marta with her towel and her bathing suit. She would still be standing by the front door, waiting for Daddy to finish loading the car, waiting with me to go charging into the back. I could sprinkle some more magic dust, and that family would swim out of their sinking car. The little kids would ride piggy-back on their daddy's shoulders as he swam against the tide, and they would all make it safely to shore.

I'd better open the window this time. Last time I forgot, and the smoke got all in the room, and I was surprised Mommy didn't smell the tobacco. If I blow it out the window and straight up, they'll never know. I'd better listen, too, because Daddy could come up the stairs while I'm blowing puffs. He might rattle the door to see that it's locked. Then he would know that something was up.

Daddy's footsteps are always soft on the hall carpet. He walks in his white socks and listens along my wall. He knows I am up to something, but he doesn't know what. So he waits out there to hear something or smell something. Sometimes when I turn down the music, I can hear him breathing.

I'm going to make sure Daddy doesn't sneak up on me on Sunday.

There's a stain on my ceiling. I never noticed it before, but just above my headboard there's this ugly yellow blotch like that amoeba on the slide in Biology, dark around the middle and spreading out.

I'm going to turn into a whore.

THE COAT CHECK GIRL

THE COAT CHECK girl at The Fountain Restaurant and Oyster Bar was rich, check it out: an average of two dollars a coat for a tip, and sometimes three, four or five when scarves, gloves, leather or mohair were involved. Eight hundred dinners on a Saturday night, do the math, the coat check girl was rich, and I was a cook, and I was not.

The coat-check girl (one of those names you always forget) wore jeans and a sweatshirt once and didn't bring a purse, so at the end of one busy shift she stuffed her pockets so tightly with her tips (four hundred ones, plus many fives and tens) that her pants looked like the stuffed mouth of a hamster. I saw her counting and organizing her tips in the break room one night (and this was a Friday, not a Saturday), and from where I was standing, there was near a thousand in front of her on that table.

One of the reasons that no one liked the coat-check girl was because no one could remember her name. It wasn't right for someone whose name you couldn't remember to make so much more than you. Even the managers were put out. I was making eight dollars an hour to cook seven-hundred dinners in one-hundred-degree heat in a heavy chef's coat. I weighed the cooking of many meals, along with the burns and the sweat and the cursing of waiters to the simple fetching of coats. From where I stood, things were clearly unfair.

Almost no one knew the coat-check girl outside of The Fountain. She talked a bit before her shift began (and never anything personal), but once it hit four o'clock, she disappeared into the back corner until people arrived or until they returned with their tickets. One of the waiters, Billy Lutz, went out for drinks with her once, but he lost interest in her after she refused to pay for her beers (why you total bitch and your many dollar bills, he related). Even Billy Lutz, after that date, mysteriously forgot her name, and he didn't have the courage after his one date (and his attitude when he left the table) to ask her to tell him it again.

Evening after evening, after she had safely put her tips away, the coat-check girl came and went alone across the parking lot and through the War Memorial. She smoked a cigarette while she walked until she disappeared between the buildings. Some saw shadows of her heading up Pine, others down Twelfth, others Rodman Alley, but where she lived remained a mystery. Like her name, she had an amazing capacity for secrecy in which direction she went in the night.

"How did she get this job? Why can't some of us check coats? Why are people tipping so much for something that takes ten seconds to get? What the hell?" Even the managers didn't seem to know, struggling through files to find her application or fishing for her punch card, which never seemed to be in a slot. Weird! It was as if she had been there in the winters checking coats all along, from before all of their times, and they were stricken powerless to replace her. One dining room manager, Pete Succhi, was so adamant about not knowing her name one evening that he walked over to her to ask her. He retrieved her name from her all right, you could see it as he held the name in the air as he strode across the dining room. But by the time he got to us at the broiler bar on the other side, he had mysteriously forgotten it. Damn!

The myth of the coat-check girl deepened when, year after year when the weather warmed and her services were no longer needed, she would disappear into the summer city, only to return when the cold weather came back and to do this one job, this one task of coat-checking that was seemingly her winter destiny. After every shift and over the years, it was always the same: the brief hellos, the retreat to the back corner of the coat room, maybe a good-bye, and then the long walk alone to wherever she was living, with only a trail of cigarette smoke to prove that she was there.

Years after my time as a cook at The Fountain had ended, I returned for dinner one snowy evening. They had left the decorations up from

Christmas, but it felt warm and familiar, except now I was going to be served and sit down in the dining room instead of cooking them myself. The menu changed, and they had more cooks, and the uniforms changed, too, and it was different too because I was older, much older, and with a life I had carved from the rest of the world. The coat-check was still in the same place, though, and I passed my houndstooth jacket and scarf over to the old woman who came into the light.

Was it her? Was it? Can I remember her face? I can't remember her name, so how can I remember her face? Shall I ask her is this you? after all this time? Were you here when I was here cooking many meals all those years back? Should I not ask her anything at all and instead just wait with my party for her to finish, ask to be excused, follow her and her trail of smoke through the War Memorial and through the back streets to finally to find out where she lives, to solve the great mystery? How much money have you made over all these years? Have you saved all of it for something profound? What have you done with the summers of your life?

Instead, as I handed over the ticket, I simply asked her for her name, because the answers to those questions I had formulated in the booth, one after the other, were no match for preserving the mystery, for letting it be, for locking away a time and a place with untold amounts of money made, a time and place swallowed up by the restaurant and the city and the past. It was another life, a life so busy with so many orders to cook, a life I no longer inhabited. So I gave the coat-check woman ten dollars, slipped on my coat, and wished her a nice new year.

After our car pulled out of the Fountain lot and onto the boulevard, I mused on her smile as she took my ticket and went for the coats. At the light, I suddenly realized that I had forgotten her name. Damn!

SLICE

TOMMY SCOTT WAS having a party again. Last year, his party involved the removal of both the front and back doors of his house in drunken stupors, and he was suspended from life by his parents for two whole months. He disappeared into the prison of his room that summer and only in the hallways the first day back to school was he able to relate his prolonged and terrible boredom. To note about the severity of Tommy's punishment: the front door was removed from its hinges reasonably enough and was put back reasonably enough, albeit loosely. No one could find the back door until the winter, however, and it was only discovered because the Lutz boy dug it up beneath some snow and leaves in the woods and tried to use it for a sled.

Tommy's father arrived with a toolbox in the hallway just after his morning coffee and unhinged Tommy's bedroom door (even though it did not fit the back and even though that door had been replaced). As a result, Tommy had no privacy, and he couldn't make much noise because the two things that could make noise, his stereo and television, had been confiscated for the summer. This troubled Tommy immensely because he had a propensity for loudness. Only when he earned enough in bus tips at Seafood Shanty would he be able to pay back the money for the back door and get back his own door. "Pay for the back door and get back your privacy and don't do it again, it's as simple as that," his mother explained.

Months removed from that wisdom, Tommy planned a bigger party. He was sure that this party was going to trump that one because his parents were going away for the weekend to a spot in the Poconos, and he spread the word effectively that the doors should, under no stupors, be removed.

Tommy planned plenty. For one, he got Bruce to bring over a big disco ball in the back of his truck, and he had streamers and such to lure the girls, and his speakers were brought down from the top room to help rumble the floors. Two kegs of beer, again off Bruce's truck, were rolled around to the side on the afternoon his parents left, hidden in the forsythia so the neighbors wouldn't draw conclusions. He brought a long table up from the basement, set up some nice cups and plates, brought liquor and glass bowls, and good food arrived from Dan and Al, the line cooks from the Shanty, who brought stolen shrimp and lunchmeat. Set up by seven, Tommy was confident, in the early hum of the music and the evening, that this night would cement his name in the Hall of Fame of Teen Parties.

Tommy had saved money beyond liquor and favors, and he spent this on an excessive amount of pizza. He called up Giuseppi's right around 8 and, filled with confidence and a pocket of cash, ordered thirty pizzas, which would work out to about two slices a party-goer. Thirty pizzas. Giuseppi explained in his broken English that it would take him until nine because "have one oven" and "make all myself." Tommy would have to pick them up because Giuseppi's take-out driver didn't come in and "no one know where he be." Giuseppi asked Tommy if he had "big car," Tommy told him yes, his friend's truck, and Giuseppi said "thirty ready at nine."

Tommy was hanging the disco ball from the top step of the stool when the headlights cut through the picture window. His knees wobbled and he sought support from the wall. He knew the high-beams: his parents had returned. Gone nearly six hours on a weekend trip, they had returned while he was standing on a stool with the Scotch tape and a handful of streamers. They were back, now what? To return to the humility of no door and no music? To incur the reputation of a cursed party host? This would be a laugh, that is what this would be.

Tommy acted quickly and valiantly in what could only be described as teen hero. It helped greatly that they sat in the driveway for ten minutes before they came in, ten minutes that Tommy later found out was spent arguing about the fleabag motel his father had booked. He grabbed the disco ball, dismounted the stool, and tore down the streamers in one circle of his arm. He carted away the speakers, wheeled away the food, folded up the table, removed the liquor and bowls, and took away the red cups. He tore upstairs to his room as they came up the walk, closed his re-instated door, and called everyone whom he had invited to cancel the whole thing. It was a work of art, his calling, with the rapid way he went through the numbers and his brief "*don't come, parents back*" message as he shaved away every would-be guest from the list. It took him thirty minutes to finish the calls. By that time, his mother and father had settled in to watching television.

They didn't notice the bits of streamer still stuck to the ceiling, or the cups left on the kitchen counter, or the trail of sawdust left on the floor from the speakers which he had dragged back to his room. Lucky for Tommy, they really didn't notice because of that horrific argument halfway up the Northeast Extension, where they took an offramp for more cigarettes, argued more, and then turned around and went south. All the while that Tommy was making his calls, he heard not a word from below. The television's volume sure was up, though, and he went down to see about things.

"Home for a reason?"

"We will talk about this another time," his father snapped.

His mother stared at the screen. It was *The Love Boat*.

"So you're not going away now?"

"No we're not and we'll talk about this another time, what did I tell you?" his father snapped again.

Music swelled on *The Love Boat*. His mother was enraged and could look at nothing but Captain Steuben. Tommy didn't know how to react at this point. Should he be peacemaker? Get them to talk about whatever turned them around and brought them back? There was that awful argument last week with the hammering of nails, his father trying to drown out his mother's bitching with "the handyman strategy": pounding while she yelled, pounding while she yelled. All of it traveled up the walls eventually, and even though they had just re-fastened his door, it didn't matter because his mother had the most piercing yell of all. Tommy couldn't shut it off even with his snazzy and expensive noise-cancel headphones.

Tommy went to the kitchen and put away the plastic cups. *The Love Boat* had a couple finding themselves again and life was grand for them now and they were giggling at the ship's railing, which didn't much match the reality of his own living room on this night. He thought about going back up to his room, but he figured he would just go out because the silence was going to end soon, he could sense it, and it was going to get ugly again. There would be things rattled and slammed the rest of the night, crying, stomping, clanging, shrieking, pretty much every noise on the auditory spectrum was going to come his way, followed by an even worse dreadful silence, so he might as well go out and get an appetizer of peace.

In the darkness behind the house, he re-hid the kegs in the forsythias, being careful that the silver barrels wouldn't shine through. There would have to be a plan for getting them out, to possibly return them to the distributor with a plea for a refund, or, if refund denied, a demented plan to drink them. Tommy hoped his parents would make up and talk again, that they would find another hotel or that his mother would accept the fleabag one. He hoped that some remnant from *The Love Boat* would seep into their lives at a commercial, change their minds, and make them take their bags out to the car and to get back giggling on the turnpike.

All of the planning and the dismantling of that planning filled Tommy's brain. This was a remarkable plan and now, a remarkable erasure of that plan; this was one he could mark down. This, in fact, might be better than having a party at all; it was all a matter of how the filled kegs would pan out, because, if the kegs panned out, it would punctuate a very good story.

But Tommy had forgotten completely about the take-out order from Guiseppi's. After he left the house, he went straight up Pelham to Rogers and into the pizzeria. Lost in thought about his silent parents and the fate of the kegs, he went up to the counter, smiled tiredly at Giuseppi, and asked for a slice, fishing for bills in his pocket. Tommy didn't notice the thirty boxes of pizza stacked against the wall. He drew a five from his pocket and felt a great sense of relief, as he placed the bill on the counter, that he would soon be able just sit down, listen to some old-time Italian music, and relax. Yes, he could just sit right down over there, across from the security guard, with a soda and a slice. He was going to sit down and eat a nice hot slice of Giuseppi's wonderful pizza and forget all of his troubles, and he was going to just sit there and munch and listen to Sinatra.

Giuseppi was sweaty and stained with pizza sauce, his hands crusted with dough, as he sliced through some mushrooms with a chef's knife on their way to a chicken marsala. Giuseppi looked up. He knew Tommy well, for Tommy had disappointed him before. Tommy had taken off on a check one day because he forgot his money and was afraid, by way of urban myth, that Giuseppi would put him to work cleaning the grease traps; and just last week, he accidentally knocked the photo of Giuseppi's mother off the wall and shattered the glass. Both times Tommy explained himself, and both times he was forgiven.

"Uh hey Giuseppi, can I have a slice?" he repeated.

Giuseppi was anticipating profit from all those pizzas and all those extras, and if Tommy had more closely observed the amount of sweat and pizza sauce on him, he might have surmised that this might be the hardest the man had ever worked, then seen the pizzas stacked along the wall, realized that he had forgotten his expensive order, and formulated a fabulous plan B for procuring them. He was oblivious, however. Giuseppi looked up, his eyes flooded with fire. Tommy was puzzled by this look, a sudden wildness he had never seen on anyone. Giuseppi stopped chopping the mushrooms.

"Slice?" Giuseppi's eyes glared in shock. "Slice? I geeva you slice!" Giuseppi leaped over the counter with his chef's knife, a leap into the air so terrifying, with knife poised in mid-air, that the security guard, sitting in his little corner booth, coughed up his Coke and spit it all over the map of Capri. Tommy took off for his life, convinced that Giuseppi had gone mad and that his stabbing was going to be the lead story on Action News. Out across the strip mall he ran, pursued a yard behind him by Giuseppi spouting long loud lines of Italian, his knife wielded to kill, and a yard behind Giuseppi, the security guard running to stop a stabbing but unable to issue a command for Giuseppi to stop because his coughing fit had not yet subsided.

Tommy made it to the construction site and hid behind the lumber that would be the Canicky's new home. The security guard caught Giuseppi in between gasps and, surprisingly, consoled him with some broken Italian. Tommy exited the other end of the lumber, relieved that his life had been spared. Nonetheless, after his heartbeats had slowed, he was still hungry for a slice. Only then did he remember his placed order of thirty pies, mumbled a *shit*, and decided that he was going to make it a point to send along a third apology, because, after all, Giuseppi made a mean pie. Thirty pizzas and two kegs were not going to go away easily, it was ridiculous to think otherwise, Tommy finally surmised. Everybody ate pizza at Giuseppi's, everybody, so his misdeed was going to spread. And two kegs may as well be two dead bodies in terms of trying to move and hide them.

The porch light was shut off when Tommy got back, unusual because it wasn't yet ten. The car was still in the driveway, so they didn't leave, and they weren't yet yelling. Tommy froze in the middle of the street, looked back, and shivered at the unusual darkness. He wondered if his earlier confrontation with Giuseppi wasn't preferable to right now. He thought about how he would enter, as if he were a burglar creeping into his own home. The night had gotten chilly and the insects that seemed so filled with noise just yesterday were now reduced to a low hum. Tommy considered his room without a door again. The summer was awful. For the first week, he could not sleep, and with no privacy and nothing to do, he had counted out time.

Instead of the security of his room and a locked door and his stereo on high if it became necessary, Tommy opted instead for a red Solo cup out of the kitchen. Fuck it, he might as well begin to put a dent in those kegs on the side yard. So he walked out to the grass and started drinking, and once he had the initial buzz, he went inside to his bedroom, closed the door, and began plan B: *come on over,* he told Bruce low over the phone, *make some calls, park your truck down the street, and bring the quiet ones with you. Spread the word to Mary Ann and Heather. Tell James and Rob to bring their cups and their pot.* This way, Tommy had a reasonable shot at polishing off one of the kegs, so long as no one made noise. His father and mother could yell all they wanted inside; in fact, with red Solo cup in hand, he was hoping for it now.

Tommy just wanted a slice of peace of mind, that's all, just a measly slice. Empty kegs would help him, by God, and with less beer in them, easier getting them safely out of the forsythias and rolled back to the distributers. Now he had something, the story he would tell about nearly losing his life to the insane stabbing Giuseppi screaming Italian across the lot. As he waited for the drinkers to arrive, he stood in the dark yard and thought about how terrible that motel in the Poconos must have been for his mother to go off like that, for his father to turn the car around and come right home. It must have been mildewed and teeming with roaches, with broken lamps and no Bibles in end table drawers, and when they started up again with the yelling inside, he concluded, as he sipped his beer, that his father deserved his mother's wrath this time because he should have known better than to book that room.

Tommy pumped another cup of beer, drinking it more quickly than the last one because the voices were rising inside the house. The light came on upstairs, and there were muffled thumps beginning. He knew the routine. He squinted into the darkness, awaiting Bruce and the rest. "He" felt relief suddenly as he sipped what was now his fourth cup, anticipating the whispered conversation and laughter to come, especially Mary Ann's low giggles. He would tell the Giuseppi story, every last detail, and implore his friends to keep it down. He would act it all out on the night grass— Guiseppi's leap over the counter, his big knife raised, his broken English, the guard coughing up his coffee all over the wall map, the desperate run across the lot to the construction site, and the shivering seclusion behind the stack of two-by-fours. Yeah, now he felt better; he had a hell of a story tell, and he could tell it and re-tell it and when the coast was clear, his friends could laugh as loud as they liked. This was one for the side yard, for the hallways, for the future. So he filled another cup and waited for his slice of happiness to arrive.

VELVET SHIPWRECKS

THEY CAUGHT ME out on one of the islands, the one between Delaware and Reed where I-95 comes in. It's a good spot because cars come slow and have to stop at the light, and the light is one of the longest in the city, so you've got plenty of time to sell before the honking starts. I had my paintings spread out across the cement; it always took me a good twenty minutes to get set up, what with the big Elvises, the same old supply of clown portraits, and of course all of the still lifes of straw flowers and such. I had to make sure the paintings faced the highway in plain view of the windshields. José taught me that two years back: big ones in the back, little ones in the front, portraits in the middle, and landscapes along the edges, so that the drivers can see what you've got before the light goes to green.

Just as I finished laying them out the police Jeep came up. It was the same one as always, K-466, flashing lights out of a pack of cars and surprising me, up over the big curb, up on the island to nail me. Fatty and Skinny, out and smiling, asked me for my solicitor's license, which of course they knew I didn't have (how many times have we been through this now?) and then started loading my paintings in the back, tossing the Elvises with no regard. "Another day another fine, ay' Domingus?" Fatty sighed. "UPS is hiring you know. You really ought to think about that."

Lucky I had the profits from yesterday's sales in my jacket. After they detained me most of the night, I sweet-talked them into giving me back my paintings after a promise that I wouldn't visit the island again. I was already thinking of where to set up (Broad and Spring Garden) and if I could get there before the morning rush. I gathered my paintings together, bound them with my elastic cords, and flung them over my back. I could hear those graveyard-shift policemen snickering across the tiles. They were going to nail me again in the very near future—they knew that, I knew that. I just hoped it wasn't today. I could make a killing today, because Friday was payday for the motorists, and that meant a weakness for paintings.

I must look like some kind of pack mule hauling these things around the city. It's impossible to get through the crowds, especially around the police station, where the sidewalks are narrow and the cabs fly by and leave you with no room. I don't know how many times I've hit people in their heads with my canvases, nailed them with the corners and pissed them off. Traveling would be easier with a car. I haven't gotten in one since the accident, and I know my insurance rates would be out the roof. But I sure wouldn't be hitting people in the heads, either. If I could work up the courage to get over things, save of some of this pocket money and get myself a car, I could make better time getting to my set-ups. Picking up my shipments would be a breeze besides.

José got a new batch of paintings in for me, some portraits of Janice Joplin and Jimi Hendrix that he said would "dazzle the eye." Of course, I had to sell what I had on my back first and that wasn't going to be easy, especially if Fatty and Skinny figured my whereabouts. The clowns weren't selling, either, and José was insistent that I get rid of some of the clowns before I picked up anything else. I don't know why clowns don't sell any more. Back in the eighties they sold like crazy. I can't remember the last time one sold. They're good clowns, too, nice even brush strokes, tastefully done, vibrant colors on good canvas. An artist named Leo did them all. He must have studied clowns for quite a bit to get those faces just right, the expressions of joy, the outright love for the world, even some pensive clowns gazing out into nowhere. And who could not like all of the colors? Reds, yellows, purples, bright blues: perfect for a kid's room or to spruce up some white walls (at least that's what I call out to the open windows). But nobody buys the clowns anymore, and I don't think it has anything to do with the art or my salesmanship. I think it's because people aren't funny anymore. They look so serious at the lights now, so grim behind their windshields. When they stop and look, it's like the weight of the world has become a decade heavier, and they've no more time for clowns.

I hadn't been to Spring Garden in nearly a year, so I lugged my paintings the ten long blocks up Broad and took a rest before unhitching my load. A pretzel vendor smiled and told me the intersection was a good one. He probably didn't remember me from last year, but I remembered him because he had said the very same thing in his Russian accent. "Lots of people come," he said. "Some will stop and buy... you'll see." Stop they did. I sold three big Elvises, a landscape and two still lifes in the first hour of the morning rush. I had forgotten how well things sold on this corner, and how the traffic flowed into the city down Broad. Normally things didn't sell quite so well in the mornings. People were tired and thinking of the workday ahead, not about paintings that might decorate the musings of their leisure time. But today they were selling. It was Friday, and money in pockets burns for leisure-time musings.

A woman in a van stopped and parallel parked in front of the vendor. She put her flashers on, dodged the traffic in her high heels, then stood on the island and surveyed my display. I don't like when people do that; she was spending too much time thinking with her fingers on her chin, and usually when people think too long, they walk away with nothing, and I wind up with nothing. Sure enough, she started back to her van, waiting at the edge of the island for the traffic to pass. I couldn't help thinking that I had just wasted another twenty minutes of my life hoping for a sell, so I had to speak up before she crossed. "Looking for something in particular?" I asked her over the roar of the engines.

"Nice work here," she shouted back. "I was hoping you had some nautical stuff."

"Nautical?" I asked. I was embarrassed to not know the word. I had heard the word but didn't know the meaning. I tried to make a connection to where I had heard it.

She moved closer so she didn't have to shout, clacking her heels on the cement. She walked back on the island and stood right in front of me. "Seascapes," she said. "I like wild, violent seascapes."

When she said 'violent" (thrusting the 'v'), I looked into her eyes. Normally I don't do that sort of thing with customers. But she said the words with such a conviction that I couldn't help but look deep into her. I saw what I saw on those clown faces in Leo's portraits, some deep, passionate resonance that rose to the surface and turned this middle-aged woman into a dream, a blonde princess of vibrant color. 'Violent' wasn't supposed to be a romantic word, a suggestive, sexual word, but here it was, laid out on the island for me, and I wanted that woman right then and there. It must have been more than the word, more than her appearance before me (a little overweight, a little dumpy, a woman in her early forties, married with a couple of kids probably, exhausted by life, nothing special to look at really). Maybe it was the morning; maybe I wanted a sale a little too much. Whatever it was, I felt compelled to move closer to her, even though a sale was out of the question.

"I . . . could get some nautical if you wanted," I said. "I have connections to any kind of art." Of course, I was lying. I was at the mercy of whatever José had to give me, and I hadn't seen a seascape come out of his supply in years. But when you're entranced, even with a dumpy, exhausted, middle-aged woman, you'll say anything to keep her interest.

She paused and looked back at her van, the flashers still going, the pretzel-man peering. "Well I come by here five days a week," she said. "I'll look for seascapes." She crossed the road in rapid clacks to avoid the rushing traffic and smiled back just before she slammed her door. I was going to lose her if I didn't come through. I'd have to find a way to get what she was looking for or she would never stop again.

Later in the day, after I packed up and high-tailed it down Ellsworth to avoid what I thought was K-466 (turned out to be another police Jeep that wasn't on to me), I set up on the island again and a man in an old Lincoln stopped and smiled at the light. This old guy started looking long and hard at the clowns. I can tell by now when I've got a sure sell coming. When a man approaches you with that light coming from his eyes, like this old man had about him, you know he's going to buy. He pulled his big car up, parked it two blocks up in a tight spot, fed the meter, and ambled over. His fingers were already on his wallet, his eyeballs fixed on the clown canvases. "I like your clowns," he said on cue. "I want some of your clowns. How much?"

Now I couldn't show him too much enthusiasm and let him know that the clowns weren't a hot commodity and that I was pushing for a sell. I had to act a little laid back, so I let him survey them on his own as I gave him a little yawn, ruffled the change in my pockets, and watched for police jeeps.

The man bought three clowns for fifty, two big happies and one of the smaller pensive ones, all of which he told me would adorn his billiards room. I didn't really care where the old guy put the things. I was just relieved to finally get rid of a few, especially two of the bigger ones. The nicest thing about selling besides the money was the load taken off your back, and those clowns were a load. It seemed as if they were on my back forever, and just to be free of them was cause for celebration. Now, as the day closed (though I only sold a landscape during the evening rush), this turned out to be one of my biggest days. I had sold ten paintings and only ten remained. Of course, my light load wasn't going to last too long, for now I could go back to José, give him his proceeds, and stock up again.

José's apartment was a disaster as usual, littered with McDonalds bags and crumpled beer cans and CD's out of their magazines. It always looked as if he had just woken from a sound sleep, even now at three in the afternoon as the sun glared through his open blinds. He brushed his hair back with his hand, kicked a bag across the room, parted some clothes scattered on his couch, and invited me to sit.

"I've got some stuff in like I told you," he said. "Seventy-five new ones in the back room. You choose. Felix was supposed to be here yesterday to pick up his shipment but got busted over in West Philly for selling bongs."

"He tried to sell them out in the open?" I asked.

"At the Student Center at Penn," José said. "He was sure that the frat boys would snap them up, and just so he could make sure of a good sell, he brought along an ounce of pot to demonstrate, the dumb fuck. Had a thick cloud around him when the cops closed in."

I knew Felix, and he wasn't one of the brightest salesmen around. Just last year, he had spent two months in jail because he stole some filet mignons from some meat purveyors and tried to peddle them to some of the busier restaurants in the city. All he had to do was take the meat out of the boxes and put them in some plain bags. But Felix left them in the boxes labeled "Wilson Meats" and then had the bad timing of selling the things just as the Wilson meat truck drove up. They had him pinned out against the dumpster—and then the cops swarmed the alley— in nothing flat. There's nothing worse than an idiot salesman, and Felix sure fit the mold.

"Well I almost got busted myself yesterday," I told José. "They got my spot pegged on the Reed island. Seems I'm running out of options."

"But you sold the clowns. That's good. There isn't much of a market for clowns these days."

"I might have found a little gold mine at Broad and Spring Garden," I said. "The traffic there. . . . "

"They nailed me there back in the day," José said. He rubbed his uncombed hair again and eyed some stale french fries scattered across the coffee table. "In fact, I don't like selling anymore because they roughed me up so good after that bust. Still feel my head against that cement."

"Well the cops don't do that sort of thing these days," I said confidently. "Rough you up I mean, what with the Rodney King fiasco and everything that followed. Bust, yeah... but I can't imagine they'd pummel me because I was selling Elvis."

"Well I've got some more dead rock stars for you," José said. He got up from his indentation in the couch, walked to the back room, and returned with two large portraits of Jimi Hendrix and Janis Joplin.

"Excuse me while I kiss the sky," I said.

"Now try to sell these as a set. The artist's name is Revlon. He gave instructions that I was to sell them as a set." José slid them in place up one of his bare white walls. "See how they complement each other? The way they face each other, looking with their glassy eyes into the abyss?"

"Glassy eyes? Abyss?"

"Look, I'm only telling you what Revlon told me. Apparently, he was painting with the conviction that they're in hell right now or something and share the same fate. He's making this statement against drugs. Feels Hendrix and Joplin set the standard."

José brought the paintings over to the couch and I inspected them. Revlon had done a nice job with the brush strokes. His color composition was good, combining muddy earth tones and black backgrounds to give an ethereal feel to the two paintings. Jimi was holding his cherry Les Paul high in the air, his Afro exaggerated to where it nearly filled the top half of the canvas as it disintegrated into the black background. Janice had this pained expression on her face, her hands clenched around a silver microphone and her mouth wide open. Her stringy, oily hair fell like water over her mashed face. I could almost hear her scream, the high pitch of a blues song, a wail of despair. Their eyes were both glassy all right; Revlon had made sure to make the pupils rise, spelling their deaths, out of the canvas with extra dabs of glossy black. I stood the paintings on the floor so that Jimi and Janice faced each other, tilting the canvases just right to let their eyes fall into Revlon's abyss.

"You're right," I said to José. "These can only be sold as a pair."

I looked at the rest of the shipment, which wasn't too impressive. He had some more landscapes with mountain ranges, some still lifes of bananas and such, some bland caricatures of Reagan and Bush riding shit-encrusted elephants, and an ugly sunflower in a wheat field.

"No more clowns?" I asked him without disappointment.

"No, Leo committed suicide."

"Suicide?" I gave an obligatory five seconds of silence and then: "how does a guy go from painting clowns to killing himself?"

"No business, Dom," José said. "You know nobody was buying the things. His last batch, hell I painted over them they were so bad. They weren't bad aesthetically...I still think Leo had a touch when it came to clowns, but he had gotten obsessed with the sad ones. Except for one smiling clown, every single one in that last batch he delivered had tears and running make-up. Depressing as hell to sit and look at them. Clowns are supposed to make you happy, that's what sold them back in the day. One poor clown even had a scar across his cheek."

"The tears of a clown when there's no one around."

"Huh?"

"Smokey Robinson," I said. I didn't want to have to explain Smokey, so I changed the subject. "Anyway, I didn't know you painted, José."

"Sure I do. Have a little art school in me. I get caught up on themes sometimes." José pulled out a portfolio from the top of his walk-in closet and unzipped it. There, covered in a layer of black dust, he retrieved a thick newsprint pad filled with charcoal drawings of tree roots, gnarled and grabbing rocks and sprouting in every direction of the paper. Several of the prints had human faces buried in the dirt, their haunting eyes obscured by a thin charcoal veil of topsoil. Others had the roots of a tree gripping the earth, strangling the continents, cracking the oceans. The drawings were hopelessly smeared, worth nothing, because José hadn't bothered to spray them."Like I said, I get caught up on themes," he said.

"So what did you paint over Leo's clowns?" I asked. "More roots?"

"Shipwrecks," he said. "I am on shipwrecks now."

That made me think of that woman who had stopped in the morning, the one who had requested 'violent' and 'nautical.' "So let me get this straight," I said. "You didn't like the depressed clowns, so you went and painted shipwrecks over them?"

"That would be right. I even painted over Leo's last happy clown."

"How is that any better, José? Isn't that more depressing?"

"I don't think it's depressing at all. Besides, it's my theme and my canvas. Leo is dead and I'm doing what I want with what he left me. I think he would be happy that I'm doing my own thing."

"Let me see them," I said.

"OK, but they're a little unusual. I painted them in a texture paint, some novel gouache they were selling down at PC Art Supply. It's paint-on velvet." He reached under his bed, pulled out the large paintings, and plopped them on the bed. There, on the top of the stack of five, was the most unusual painting I had ever seen. The paint, of deep greens and whites and muddy browns, seemed to be growing wild out of the canvas like mold, rising a half-inch off the surface.

"What the hell?"

"Synthetic velvet. I've never seen anything like it," José said.

I rubbed the surface, and the fuzzy texture moved under my thumb as if it were alive. It sure felt like velvet. I picked up the painting, held it at arm's length, and examined the ship going down. It had splintered, like his tree roots, the length of the canvas. Shards of broken wood were being thrown, the mast had snapped in half, and the survivors, rising up off the canvas, clung to bits of broken ship.

"Now bear in mind that I know a little about shipwrecks."

"The way you know about tree roots strangling the planet?"

"Seriously," he pointed, "this one here is the Annie Jane, an emigrant vessel shipwrecked off the coast of Scotland in the nineteenth century. Two hundred fifteen died."

I looked closer and saw the women and children suffocating in wet shawls and clinging to the broken mast. Little white gouaches of terror, flicked by José's brush, sprung from their corneas. All around them the waves rose like dark massive buildings, steel blue waves tipping, tipping, ready to crush them.

"How do you know about shipwrecks?" I asked him.

"Had a special on one of the cable channels. Took my interest. Took notes. Thought of Leo's shitty clown paintings right away and got out my black velvet paint and covered them all over."

I lifted the painting to see another dark shipwreck, what looked like a steamboat burning in a river. I could see the gray velvet cypresses barely visible in the background, and, within the tall flames, José had painted, to the top of the canvas, little soldiers jumping overboard, each on fire. The ship itself, ablaze, was sinking in the glassy river, as the water gushed over the deck, as it tilted and spilled hundreds over its side.

"The Mississippi sidewheeler Sultana," he said. "Worst marine disaster in U.S. history." José picked up the painting and angled it into the light of his open blinds, so that I could see the detail of the burning bodies working to extinguish themselves in the river. "A bunch of Union soldiers, over 2,400, had just been released from Confederate prison camps...the war was over, and they were happy and celebrating their peaceful futures, all full of Southern Comfort." José brought the painting back to the bed. "There were a hundred civilians on board, too."

I looked and saw, bobbing in the river, a number of animals' heads—horses, mules, pigs swimming in frantic painted circles and pawing the water.

"Animals? And is this what I think it is? a giant alligator breaking out of a crate?"

"Yeah, they had a cargo of farm animals on the Sultana and a ten-foot alligator which escaped from its crate and killed two soldiers as they burned. Another desperate soldier, who apparently couldn't swim, killed the alligator and used the crate to float to safety."

"What happened?" I asked. "To cause the fire?"

"Boiler exploded. Right in the middle of their party, as they were cheering 'north north north north,' the thing blew. I painted the sidewheeler about thirty seconds after it exploded. Wanted to catch the terror, the flames the way they were at that moment."

I stood and stared at the horror, fascinated by the human and animal bodies mingling in the dark river. José had put some work into this one with his fine brushes, and the velvet made the black water rise up out of the canvas. The flames, so bright against the backdrop of gray cypresses, seemed to flicker into reality. The detail was incredible.

"Over 1550 lives lost," he said. "Worse than the Titanic."

"José, I want to sell these for you. Let me sell your shipwrecks." I picked up the second painting and looked at the other three that he had painted as he explained each of them: the Queen Mary ramming and sinking a British cruiser, a Canadian Great Lakes cruise ship burning at a dock, and a minesweeper colliding with an aircraft carrier. In each of the remaining three, José had made sure to meticulously work in the dying passengers, filled with terror, into the raging waters with the tip of his fine brush.

"I think I've got an instant sale on some of these," I said. "A woman stopped this morning looking for nautical."

"Well I wouldn't call these typical nautical," José said. "She was probably looking for seascapes, non-velvet seascapes."

"You don't know what you've got here," I told him. "I'm no art critic, but I know what sells. I set myself up on Spring Garden and this lady will come. These aren't clowns you've got here. These things will jump out at the rush hour traffic."

"Well in a way they are clowns," José smiled. "Under all this fake velvet, remember, you've got some pretty serious clowns—tears and scars and Leo speaking from the grave." José put his hand on the paintings and looked over at me. "I never sold anything of my own. Never thought anything I did could sell. Hell, you saw my charcoal roots, all smeared and useless. My craftsmanship has always pretty much sucked up until this velvet paint." He smiled and admired his new work on the bed. "I have to admit I did a nice job of keeping things neat this time around."

I talked him into letting me sell three of the paintings, though he wanted to hold on to the Sultana. and the Annie Jane. "This one with the animal heads is your masterpiece, though", I said. "You could get a hundred for this one."

"I put a lot of work into it," he said, cradling the big thing to his chest. "I'm not about to have it sold out on one of the islands. Maybe I want to keep it for my own."

I rummaged through his new stock and found a few more still-lifes, strapped the load to my back, and headed out the door. "I can sell these three for fifty apiece, that's for sure," I said. "Soon you'll be eating better than McDonalds." I kicked a crumpled bag in my path and braced my back with the new load.

Out on the island, just before the sun comes up and just before the traffic hits, I get a special feeling of peace, a quietness not unlike sitting on a hilltop watching a valley come out of a fog. I could see a batch of headlights several blocks up as I circled my display around me and I made sure to put José's shipwrecks at the center. I guess I was expecting something special today, even though it was a Monday and Mondays are usually slow. Maybe I felt some extra power in my display, that same invigorating feeling I always get after a new stock. After all, the clowns were gone—replaced by José's shipwrecks—and now people were going to slow down and take a more serious look. I stepped into the street and looked at the velvet coming at me from the island, trying to see what the buyers might see as they sat behind their windshields. Even in the dim early light, where it was difficult to see things from a distance clearly, I expected something more. I waited for those same visions I had received under José's open blinds, those desperate victims rising so real off the canvas. But there wasn't enough light to do that yet; the shipwrecks, in fact, didn't stand out at all and looked mostly dull and black from a distance. People weren't going to look seriously in this light. I needed the sun.

Just after seven, after the sky had brightened the island, I saw her van in the other lane, coming quick to the light. It was her all right, but she was going too fast to spot the shipwrecks and it was too late to wave her down. The light stayed green and she flew by the pretzel vendor, and I sighed and cursed and looked around for other curious eyes. I picked up Revlon's masterpieces and held them up in the light, flashing them to the cars that slowed as the light finally turned red. "Hendrix and Joplin right here," I called out with dying conviction. "Remember the sixties with these two."

I sold nothing during the rush, not one blasted painting. As the cars thinned, I looked across the island to the other side of the street, where the pretzel vendor had squeezed the top of his body out of his aluminum hole. He shrugged his shoulders over the last of the passing cars, as if to say 'well this doesn't look like a good day to sell, for you or for me, but what can be done?' He pulled back into his metal shell and opened a can of soda.

The paintings were heavy today, and I could feel a knot beginning at the bottom of my back. Back problems happen a lot anymore, especially at the beginning of the week when I've got a full load to haul. I thought about my old car, mangled and worthless over at the scrap yard. The tires were still good, and somebody had probably come along and salvaged the bucket seats by now, maybe even taken the Die-Hard off its terminals.

I had heard about some right-wing radical group making weapons out of car battery acid, something on the TV or in a newspaper, I didn't remember which. They probably had found all of their ammunition in salvage yards and under hoods of mangled cars just like mine. Maybe somebody, right as I was standing on the island trying to sell paintings, was building a bomb out of my old battery.

It's been almost a year since the accident, but it still comes back clear as mountain air. I'm convinced I'll never be able to shake the image of that woman and her flowers toppling over the hood, or the heavy thud tumbling over the roof, or her lifeless body spilling over my back window to the pavement. The sting of her death went like a needle into my brain at that moment—I'll never forget that moment—and then the telephone pole came up, materialized right there, right in front of me out of my fog. All I could do was hold on—I'm still holding on—as I braced for impact, as I closed my eyes to the imploding windshield, as I closed my eyes at the thought of the dead woman, with her spilled roses, somewhere behind me. I remember thinking that it didn't much matter to me whether I lived or died at my moment of impact. I was only thinking of the woman as I hit the pole. When I awoke some days later in Lankanau hospital, they told me my face would be all right, and my broken arms would heal, and that after a few days— and a lot of questions—I could leave. I told the investigators, in my delirium, that she had walked right out in front of me, out from the darkened trolley tracks and right into the middle of the road. That short little woman, busy trying to cross the road and sell her armload of roses, didn't even see me—nor did I see her—until it was too late. The investigators talked in corners, came back, and told me that it wasn't my fault. They asked me to stop crying and assured me that it wasn't my fault. "She had very bad eyesight," one of them said. "She didn't see you coming, Domingus."

I don't know if I'll ever drive again. I'd like to get the courage up sometime soon so I don't fear it forever, and it sure would make my load easier to transport. I'm usually careful when I cross the road with my paintings, though with all of my bending over that can be difficult. Sometimes I don't see things when they creep up on me. Just last week a guy nearly hit me coming up Rhawn, then leaned out his window and told me to watch myself.

The afternoon came up fast. Sometimes, especially when I'm preoccupied, the day moves in a blur and the cars come and go—without a sound it seems—as I get lost in my past, as I get caught too long at my moments of impact. Wasn't it just the morning rush? Wasn't I just squinting in the middle of the road to get a distant view of my shipwrecks? Now the sun had swung clear up past the middle of the sky and had begun its descent into a forest of buildings. The traffic thickened again, and through the drone I heard a horn go off. I turned to see the white van pulling up along the vendor.

"I see you've remembered me," she called out over the passing cars. She put on her flashers, smiled, and clacked in rapid leaps to the island.

"I've got your nautical," I said. "Some very unusual nautical."

She surveyed, again with her hands on her chin. She stood on the edge of the cement and I watched as her eyes widened, and then as she reached to touch. I was sure of this one. I had myself a sell.

"Velvet paint," I said. "José used a very special gouache."

"These are what I've been looking for," she said. She squatted and ran her finger through the velvet. "You're right, unusual," she said. "You know the artist?"

"José Miranda," I said. "He usually just gets me my stock from other artists, but he did these ones on his own." I didn't tell her about the clowns painted beneath; clowns, on the surface or beneath it, didn't sell.

"What a paradox," she said.

Paradox—another word, just like 'nautical,' that was working my brain into a giant question.

"Velvet shipwrecks," she said, almost in a whisper. "Usually when artists use velvet, it's to convey something pleasant. Velvet is usually used for portraits and still-life. But your José has done a remarkable job satirizing the public's glorification of disasters by using velvet on shipwrecks." She got up from her squat and moved close. "How much?"

"Fifty apiece," I said. "José insisted I sell them for no less. He worked long and hard..."

"I'll take all three," she said quickly. I should have asked for more because she bought too soon. She crossed the street for her pocketbook and returned with a wad of bills. "I'd appreciate it if you could load them in my van for me," she said.

I stuffed the bills in my pocket and carried the velvet shipwrecks across, loading them into her van after she opened the sliding door. A van—this would be perfect for me if I ever decided to drive again. I could take José's entire supply—seventy-five paintings—and fit them in the back. I could just open my van and let people rummage, park up on any sidewalk in any part of the city and line them up. With that kind of choice, people would look for me, and I could sell wherever I wanted. I could even get a sign on the side, "Dom's Art" or something, maybe have José paint some tree roots to get their attention.

"I'd like more shipwrecks if you could get them," she said as she slammed the sliding door.

"José has two more," I said. "One of them is incredible, of the sidewheeler Sultana burning in the Mississippi River." She stopped and looked at me: I could tell she was impressed with my knowledge.

"Whatever he paints I'll buy," she said. "Tell him to keep painting shipwrecks, tell him to keep using that unusual gouache." Reaching deep into her purse, she pulled out a business card and handed it over. "I'm Maureen. You call me when you've got more. And don't you dare sell any of those shipwrecks to anyone else." She smiled again and left me wanting her as she lifted her dumpy frame into the van. She waved and pulled away, and the vendor squeezed out of his hole and raised his thumbs into the air.

As I re-arranged the paintings, placing Hendrix and Joplin in the spot of the empty shipwrecks (making sure to create Revlon's abyss), K-466 came roaring up behind me. I don't how they're able to do that—appear out of thin air in such a big vehicle. I always try to be cautious and watch for them, look all four ways at the intersection every thirty seconds or so. But it seems as soon as I look away for more than that, they roll up on the island. They must have some kind of trick they use, something they learned at the academy.

"All right Domingus, this was your last straw," Skinny said. "Unless you got yourself a solicitor's license over the last three days, you're coming back to the station."

Fatty was flinging my paintings hard into the back of the jeep. He stepped on the Bush caricature and cracked the frame clean in half.

"Hey you're breaking my stuff," I shouted.

"Well your stuff doesn't matter this time my friend," he said. "This time you're not getting any of it back." He picked up the Reagan and studied the grimacing ex-president sitting on his shit-encrusted elephant. "Somebody doesn't like Republicans, does they?"

"I know you've heard this before, but I promise I won't sell any more," I said hollowly. "I've got money invested in these..."

"You sure won't cause you'll have nothing to sell," Skinny said. "This batch is now property of the city."

I could feel the eyes of the rush hour watching me at the light, eyes behind windshields that, moments earlier, might have been looking to buy. Now they were gawking at my misfortune. Fatty had been eyeing the Hendrix and Joplin the whole time. I watched as he carefully slid them in on top of the others. I was sure he was going to claim them for his own— he already had a spot picked out on one of his bare walls.

"Careful with the head. You know the routine," Skinny said, opening the side door and guiding me in. I yawned and buried my head in my hands, cursing the broken Bush and my confiscated load.

"They didn't give nothing back?" José shouted across the room. "You lost them all?" He tossed a pair of pants clear past the end of his couch and sighed with all his breath. I pulled out the wad of bills given to me by the woman and waved it in the air. "Except for your shipwrecks, José," I said. "Here's the money for your shipwrecks."

Just like that, José stopped his sighs, smiled, and snatched the wad. He counted it and patted me on the back. "Well it's not a total loss then," he finally said.

"I need you to let me sell the other two," I said. "This woman gave me her card and wants to buy as many as you can paint." I flashed her business card and returned it to my pocket. "We could sell them for a hundred apiece easy. We could make a nice living off this woman, you and me."

"I've bought some more canvas and frames, you know," José said. "When I got those tree roots down out of the closet the other day, it inspired me about painting things again. I've got some pretty decent craftsmanship now."

"You're an artist damnit," I said. "So paint more shipwrecks. I need to stay off the street for a while besides. They got me pegged."

I called Maureen that evening and she answered on the first ring. I identified myself as 'the guy on the island who sold you shipwrecks' and told her I had a few more. "José's going to paint for you," I said. "As many shipwrecks as you want."

She told me to keep them coming and gave me directions to her home in northeast Philly, where she was willing to pay a hundred apiece for the Sultana and the Annie Jane. Even though the bust cost me a nice profit, I was relieved that I didn't have to lug my load around for a while, nor worry about the police hunting me down. Really, though, I was thinking about Maureen: did she have a husband, a family? why was it she who answered the phone? why on the first ring? I couldn't help thinking we had made a connection, a connection beyond the shipwrecks, back there on the island. I couldn't help thinking that she was sending signals.

I had to take the C bus clear up Broad, transfer at Hunting Park, and transfer again to a bus up the boulevard. Lucky for me the bus was near empty, because José's shipwrecks took up half the aisle and you couldn't get past them. Some of the scattered passengers looked back and admired them, and I could see the bus driver, a four-hundred-pound man easily, eyeing me in the rear-view mirror, flashing a look of suspicion that had me already convicted as an art thief.

Maureen's row home sat three blocks off the boulevard in Feltonville, behind a wall of thick hedges that ran the entire street. I rang her bell and stepped back, suspecting that she would answer on the first ring. I saw her hand part the drapes, and when she opened the door, the aroma of fresh flowers hit me like a wall. It reminded me of a funeral parlor. It reminded me of the dead woman and her spilled roses. I gathered the shipwrecks under my arm and waited as her fingers unhitched the lock.

"Hello, come on in," she said. She was standing there in tight jeans and a Phillies t-shirt and looked up and down the street as she opened the door wide. The tight jeans gave her heavy hips away, though she didn't seem to care. Perhaps that was what made her all that more appealing. I followed her in and her hand brushed my shoulder as I walked the long carpet.

I was expecting vases filled with roses and gladiolas and daisies strung around her living room, perhaps some exotic arrangement rising from her coffee table. But I didn't see one flower, not one.

"I smell flowers. Where are the flowers?"

She smiled and whispered "air freshener" (making me think that she had sprayed for me), then invited me to sit. I thought that she would attack the paintings as soon as I rested them against the wall, inspect her two new shipwrecks and forget all about me. Instead, she asked me if I wanted a drink.

"I know you've come a long way and I didn't hear you drive up. You took the buses?"

"Yes, I don't have a car." I didn't want to get into that. "If you've got a beer," I said quickly.

She went to her refrigerator and I surveyed her living room—the worn couch and chair, the stained carpet, some assorted photographs of boys on football teams, some floral curtains covering the windows. No pictures on the walls at all. Some tack holes that need to be spackled, but no pictures at all. I got up off the couch and checked the darkened walls of her staircase in search of the other three shipwrecks, in search of any art. Was she alone here? Could I hear any other voices behind closed doors at the top of the stairs? I strained my ears.

"Hope you don't mind domestic cans," she said, handing me a Miller.

"Not at all," I sipped, and then with my eyes pointing, "take a look at José's shipwrecks."

She walked to the wall and spread the paintings apart, dropping to her knees to inspect the flailing bodies strewn across the black velvet water. "A riverboat," she said. "A burning riverboat." She stepped back, moved the pole lamp into place so that it caught the velvet rising off the canvas, the terror of the burning soldiers. Long shadows cast themselves upward and the ceiling moved with light. I sipped my beer and watched as her hand moved across the surface of the two paintings.

"These are so beautiful," she said in a whisper.

She turned to me and watched as I emptied the Miller and prepared my historical explanation. Then she moved closer to the couch as I explained the fate of the Sultana. I finished telling her about the large alligator, and she asked me up the stairs. "I want you to see how I've arranged the first three," she said.

In her room, up over her dark headboard, she had mounted her three velvet shipwrecks so that the frames touched each other. It reminded me of Revlon's Hendrix and Joplin in the way that they complemented each other, all ships sinking together on the same black sea into an infernal abyss.

"If you step back here," she said, pulling me by the arm and taking me to the front of her dresser, "and turn down the light, well you can almost imagine you're in there, swimming among them."

In the silence of her gaze, I moved my eyes to her bed—half-made, a pillow almost falling from the far end—and thought of her again, and suddenly I became sensualized there in her bedroom. I could feel her shoulder touching mine and I moved my hand toward her back.

"You're married?" I asked.

"No longer," she said. "My husband left me six years back."

I had walked into a hornet's nest with my question and instinctively moved my shoulder away.

"Oh well I'm..." I was going to apologize but then finished, "who were those football pictures?"

"My two sons," she answered. "Those pictures are ten years old. My boys are off at college now. University Park. Off and gone." She paused and gazed heavily into the shipwrecks. I had ventured much too far into her personal life and I could feel her sinking into an ooze of silence. I wanted to scramble from the room, tell her I had to leave and head back to the buses. After all, who was I but some poor, luckless street peddler? I had stepped into this woman's life only to deliver some paintings, and now I had finished my Miller and I was done. Who was I to step any further? But I couldn't tear myself away—she held me in her force field, as her eyes, transfixed upon the velvet sea—that calamitous velvet sea—forced me to wait out the silence.

"The son of the bitch never came home," she said.

"Never came..." She broke her stare and turned to me. "I'm sorry, I didn't mean to dump this on you."

"Please dump," I said, touching her arm. "I'll listen."

"My husband Eddie went away on a boat," she said. "Last summer he took a trip on the tall ship Gazela."

"The one docked at Penn's Landing?" I asked. I had seen a tall ship come and go there.

She nodded. "He always wanted to work as a crew hand on a tall ship. The first mate hired him to cook the meals for the whole crew. They trained him how to set the sails. They were taking the Gazela back to Portugal for her one-hundredth birthday and there was going to be a celebration all along the docks there. Eddie, he wanted to sail for his fortieth birthday, he wanted it more than anything. We talked about it and I let him go." Maureen sat down on the end of her bed and the springs squeaked. "I let him go."

I looked at the sinking ships, then back to her. "He never came back?"

"My guess is that he met a Portuguese woman after they docked in Setubal. Or maybe he had a little plan all along—a secret plan to keep on going—and high-tailed it across Europe. He always wanted to ski the Alps, he always wanted to wander behind the old Iron Curtain."

Now I knew why the woman wanted José's shipwrecks: she was wishing him dead, right up there on her wall. She was wishing his ship sunk. She wanted the Gazela crushed and split open by iron waves, taking him down into the cold, into the thick velvet sea. Up on her wall, up over her dark headboard, each one of those passengers—the women, the children in shawls, the navy men scrambling, and then down in her living room—the burning soldiers, even the bobbing animal heads—each was a thousand nights cursing her husband, cursing his one-way voyage, cursing his new life.

Then I figured out why I liked them, too. I stared back at the wall as she sighed. Then I sighed too, for I knew why I had come. To sell José's paintings, sure. To get two hundred dollars, sure…but also to sell myself to Maureen. For those shipwrecks were me, too. They were the dead woman and her spilled roses, they were the impact of the telephone pole, they were the sleepless nights and the tears shed in front of those detectives and the sound that sometimes wouldn't go away, the sound of the thud that was not unlike the sound of a ship going down. The shipwrecks were me and the shipwrecks were her. That's all there was as we both fell into the silence of the room.

She must have expected me to come over to her there on the bed, to touch her arm like I did, to take her chin and pull her in and kiss her. I didn't need to tell her anything, I didn't need to dump my accident out there or work up a face full of tears. She knew that I knew all about shipwrecks, that buried within me—as in her—were a thousand screams of a thousand drowning souls. When we kissed, it was to let each other know that we would make it through, both of us together, as we held to bits of broken ship. We saw the shoreline appear from out of the abyss of each other's eyes, and we were going to be the lucky ones.

José painted the H.M.S. Birkenhead, the largest iron ship in the Royal Navy, sinking just after it had struck a rock off Danger Point. On the deck of the ship, the troops had dressed in full uniform, falling in in rigid ranks to beating drums while the women and children paddled off in boats. The water had risen to their waists in the painting, and José was careful to paint the men staring straight ahead as the ship tilted for its ride downward. With their faces stern and unfeeling, some of the men shook each other's hands farewell, as if just another day was coming to a close. All around the ship the sharks had gathered, flashing their velvety white teeth and their sleek gray bodies, waiting for the men to drop as the sea rose up.

"Used up a lot of velvet gouache on this one," José said. "Be sure to sell it to Maureen for at least a hundred."

I wasn't about to charge her a hundred, though I didn't want to let José know that. I knew Maureen had lost a little interest by now and had moved the paintings from above her bed down to the living room walls. I had just talked to her on the telephone and she had complained that one of the paintings was losing velvet. She was making dinner tonight and would only hint that it was to be a surprise.

Maureen's van needed gas, so I stopped and filled it with high octane before heading back to Feltonville. It cost me twenty dollars, but I figured it was the least I could do for her. After all, she was letting me haul my load, and I was driving again, really driving. She was standing before the Sultana when I arrived, running her fingers across the surface.

"Come see this Dom," she said. I kissed her, rubbed her back, kissed her again, and looked close. She had begun to peel away chunks of velvet from the center of the painting. "I noticed some flecks on the floor this morning," she said. "This painting is losing paint. And there's something underneath."

I reached up, pinched away a bit of the clinging velvet, and peeled it away. A good two inches of dried black gouache fell into my hand like a scab. Frantically, we worked together with our fingers to remove the loose paint from the canvas. José's craftsmanship wasn't so good after all, I kept thinking. He probably hadn't sprayed, and I figured that all of his velvet shipwrecks, somewhere down the line, were going to fall to the floor in heaps of ash.

We peeled away a large circle in the middle of the canvas as it spread outward like a cancer. Maureen stopped her peeling and stepped back to get a better view. "It's a clown I think," she said and put her fingers to her chin. "I can see the face."

I stepped back, took her hand, and looked. Sure enough, I saw the powdered white cheeks, the big blue reflecting eyes and the wide, red-lipped smile of a clown within the chipped-away circle. The eyes sparkled through, and the lips, thick and prominent, rose like a beacon out of the dark, flecked-away sea.

Leo, with his last happy clown, was speaking from the grave, whispering his secret message from beneath the velvet. He must have been smiling, too, just like his clown. He must have been smiling just like me as I turned, closed my eyes, and kissed Maureen.

ONLY LOSS

DAD MISSED ANOTHER weekend, this time because his engine needed an overhaul. Before that, he broke three toes on his right foot getting a beer ball down from the shelf at Holstein's Distributors, and before that he had the flu. It was always something, and it was becoming more and more something every time every other weekend rolled around. "He will never be the father you want him to be," Mom would sigh on cue the moment he was breaking a promise over the phone. "He is, was, and always will be, a day late and a dollar short."

Dad had promised me, from the time I was six to the time mom left him when I was twelve, tickets to go see the Globetrotters. After the divorce and on one of the few weekends that the world did not conspire against dad and block his way to me, he picked me up one Friday after school and held two Globetrotters tickets up to the afternoon light. "Like I promised you I would."

Dad's talk on the ride back to his efficiency (and the crappy cot with the rusting springs on which I slept) was all about the amazing acrobatics and the spinning basketballs, crazy dunks, fabulous layups, players on each other's shoulders, and that he could finally deliver me a promise that could never be broken: a great time filled with trick plays, and a certain win. "You're not going to believe what they can do," he promised.

"The Globetrotters have never lost," he said. "Never. I promise you they will not lose. I promise you we will win." This did not sound like the man, bankrupt of certainty, I had come to know as dad. It was as if the mishaps that had shaped his life up to this moment has passed away and meant nothing now. Curly Neal, Sweet Lou Dunbar, and Meadlowlark

Lemon would save the day and erase all of the years before that day, redeem his unfulfilled promises with fancy layups and blindfolded mid-court shots.

We traveled from Nashville to the town of Martin, Tennessee to see them play. Over the course of the long ride, I was promised a fun time sitting in the stands, with, among other things, buckets of water that would "accidentally" be splashed our way. "You're going to get soaking wet," dad laughed, and then, "but don't worry, management will provide towels."

There was no splash and no need for towels. Every promised trick play was at the other end, with even the shoulder-stands impossible to see because of two tall men with bulbous heads sitting in front of us, neither of whom seemed to care about enjoyment. I could hear other kids laughing and reveling in the tricks and splashes, but not us, not us hidden behind the heads. The other team, the Reds, wore blood-red uniforms. I'll never forget the blood-red uniforms. There is nothing I remember about trick shots from the Globetrotters except through video highlights on the television, but even today I remember the blood-red uniforms of that other team.

The Globetrotters were supposed to put teams away by forty points, but in this particular game they were up by only a point with ten seconds left. Dad complained because the owner of the Reds was playing in the game, which for some reason to him was unfair. To make things much worse, this owner-player made the layup that put the Reds in front with three seconds left. Dad stood up and yelled down to the court, visibly shaken by the basket, and the Day-Late-And-A-Dollar-Short Gods seemed to be moving in again; the Black Cloud moved across the arena and right over our heads, ready to rain disappointment.

The concerned timekeeper stood below us and there were confused whispers in the stands as we entered this suddenly new universe for the team that had never ever lost. All of the acrobatics and ball-spins, all of the whistlings of "Sweet Georgia Brown," and all of the standings-on-shoulders and blind mid-court shots in the world would not contain enough magic for a win, even with the Globetrotters staunch ally the timekeeper. Tricks take more than three seconds to set up, and dad told me that none of the players had ever trained on desperation throws. "Why would they?" he muttered.

"But the timekeeper will save them, right, dad? They are supposed to win, so the timekeeper will save them. Right? Your promise, right? For all of the broken ones?"

I looked up and there were zeroes. I looked into the stands, not to my father, for explanation. Other kids, some assembled in large groups with adult chaperones, started crying section by section like an infection. Angry adults booed and yelled for extra time. On the floor the players, especially the Reds, were in confusion, and then, out of mere obligation, they celebrated by patting shoulders and butts in front of a ripped-off crowd. Quietly, the timekeeper packed up his box and left the table.

Now, LONG AFTER the falling-out with dad, the gulf of years, and his quiet funeral, that Globetrotters only loss has returned with force. The slow ticking of the clock, the zeroes above us, the click click of the timekeeper packing his box, all imprinted a time, place, and circumstance that will never exist again. Now, with dad's funeral, the wound has been unearthed. Never did the Globetrotters lose again after that loss; the universe would make sure of it, history would make sure of it. Now, I hold their only loss bitterly in the forefront of memory as I make my way through the mourners and say my indifferent good-bye to my father's body on the kneeler. It is solely my defeat now.

My mother died just about three years ago; she never married after dad, and there was a perpetual sadness to her in those last years, especially after the cancer took away her body and filled in the holes with heavy regret. My sister, who arrived to dad's funeral from the coast with her husband and children in tow, and whom I hadn't seen in eight years, provided a little conversation at the reception, and even a little laughter about earlier times, but I pretty much didn't know anyone else save for a stray uncle, and I felt the heavy day of that loss again, so I slipped out unseen.

I stopped in at the Aztec Pub after the funeral because I badly needed some drinks. The bar was crowded and there was a row of men watching a Sixers-Celtics game on the big screen. After I finished my first beer, and during the commercial, and because it was still in the forefront of my memory, I brought up the Globetrotters game. "I was at the only Globetrotters game they ever lost," I said to them, drawing their eyes toward me. "I was in the stands that day."

I could tell they were big Celtics fans because they had been shouting at the screen from the moment I walked in, but after I began telling my story, and even after the game returned from commercial break, they wanted to hear more about the only loss. Their Sixers-Celtics game suddenly didn't matter to them anymore, their collective attention was on me now, so I told them everything about the game, being careful to leave the disappointment that was my father out of the narrative.

"Wow, how lucky you were to see them lose," the bearded man on the corner said. He stood up and motioned to the end of the bar, where a couple was sitting. "Hey Jeff and Nancy, this guy here saw the only Globetrotters game they ever lost." The couple perked up, gathered their drinks, and came down to join us. I had a story to tell, and all of them wanted to hear about the game again, as more gathered, as those in the booths took a listen. I told them about the owner of the Reds actually playing in the game and making the final shot, about the futile desperation throw from Curly, about the confusion on the floor and in the stands after the unthinkable had happened, about the throngs of children in tears, about the perplexed timekeeper just below me sighing and packing up his box. After I finished the story, there was a collective wow.

Later in the evening, after more than enough beer, I laid on the couch and wondered what I would have seen had I looked to dad in the moments following that loss. Instead of watching the other kids cry that day, because I was so angry at another broken promise, what if I had looked to dad right then and there? Would I have cried then like the other kids? Would I have cried for him? I didn't want to look at him, though. I knew the game was over, and I was angry at him because he had broken another promise, perhaps the biggest promise of all, the one he held firm in his hand for six whole years of my childhood, and then, when it arrived, he handed me instead an utter letdown. Now, after I told the story at the Aztec Pub, it wasn't about the loss anymore, about disappointment anymore, it was about the story.

How was I to know that the stories of all of my father's promises were never meant to be broken ones? That he was a man always down on his luck, and that this indelible moment of time, place, and circumstance drove a lasting wedge into his efforts to be a good father? Dad would make too many more promises that he would never keep, of course, something he seemed resigned to do, and it was the eventual person into which he settled, but my story of him was always about failure until now. It was always about failure until I visited the Aztec Pub after his funeral. For all those years, I had held dad to those broken promises across the rest of his life, dismissed the very idea that it was the bad luck and only the bad luck, or a man simply lacking the genetics of responsibility. Now, after drinks and conversations with strangers at a bar, I realize that bad luck was indeed the driving force that prevented him from being the father he could have been, and the times we could have had, with even a sprinkle of fortune.

In retrospect that's now ok, so I carry January 25, 1971 and that three-hour game like a feather. It has become a moment of luck finally. I tell the story almost every time I sit down at a bar when the topic of basketball comes up, at my job, and I even wrote a blog about that game in Martin, Tennessee that got over two hundred likes. And sometimes conversations carry on beyond the game. I have made some new friends, Jackie and Janice, with those extended conversations, and Jackie introduced me to Eileen, arriving so late in my life, who will soon become my wife. In my history of being there for sports history, those three hours with dad when I was twelve are now immortalized: they have opened the door to the good times I had with my dad and to the good times now, good times that were there all along, but always shrouded by his disappointments.

Not anymore. Now they have steered me here. Now, when I think about the time we were stuck atop the Ferris wheel because someone below had dislodged a plug, I think not of the bad luck being at the very top, but of the beautiful, cool summer night we spent swaying there in our seats, closer to the moon than anyone else on the ride. Or when Dark Hollow Road was closed for construction when dad wanted to take me there, on one of his Sundays with me, to show me the stone bridge what was supposedly haunted by ghosts, we took a ride instead out of the way and got way lost, and I got home late and mom was mad because it was a school night, but we got to see a flock of Whooping Cranes ascend to the sky from the brown fields on both sides of the lost road, and all of them flew splendidly across a large pale setting sun in a glorious display of white flapping wings, tip to tip. Now I vividly remember those majestic birds and how they all glided away there in a wave of beauty off of the brown fields.

Dad is dead, but dad is a new man. I am a new man, too, filled with new memories and promises of more new memories as the leaks gather on my wall of disappointment, as memories flood in, as the wall finally begins its crumble. That Globetrotters loss was the only time in my life that I would go to a Globetrotters game, it was the only Globetrotters loss anyone would ever witness, and I was with my dad. How lucky is that?

DOUBLE YELLOW

EDGAR STRAPPED HIS mother in good, the way she always insisted. He made sure to pull the seat belt out and release it so it tightened against her frail chest. "Don't you forget yours," she told him as he walked around the back of the car. "They don't put them in for no reason and they don't pass laws for no reason."

Edgar only used the belt when his mother rode as passenger. It was beige and it was uncomfortable. He tried to reach casually to his left as if it was something he always did but fumbled blindly with his hand until finally he had to turn and look for the restraint. His mother watched the whole clumsy contrivance behind thick lenses some worried doctor had prescribed.

"You really ought to wear your seat belt at all times, Edgar. You might think it's no big deal driving like hell all alone and I know you drive fast like that Andretti fellow and I know you think you're getting away with something but God help you if you should crash" came the motherly soliloquy, "because your car might stop but you'll just keep going seventy miles an hour or however fast you drive and you can have a crash helmet and a suit of armor on for all I care but it's not going to do a damn bit of good. You'll be dead all over the road."

Edgar was going to lie to her about wearing his seat belt, but she'd seen thirty-three years of his act. She started in on him about sons lying to their mothers, and how it related to the article spread across her Daily Trentonian, the article with the photo of the moustached man and how he had just blown up a Colonial bi-level after the family had driven away to Sunday Mass and in the arresting photo he had smirked at the camera. She talked about the meaning of that smirk, the similarity that peculiar kind of look had to Edgar during the times "when he was thinking too long". The gruesome comparison made Edgar fidget for a distraction. He went to turn on the radio, then remembered it didn't work and pulled his hand back.

"Sometimes I forget to wear the thing, Ma," he said. "With quick trips sometimes you don't think."

"With quick trips you die. I've seen the statistics."

Edgar was taking her to Aunt Rita's row home over in Mayfair, a thirty-minute drive by way of Hulmeville Road. Alone, or with Sammy and Skipper, Edgar would normally cruise that road with a cold imported beer and let the wind suck itself in the windows and make the trees fly by in a green blur.

"Be careful on this road, Edgar, " his mother said, pointing her bony finger out the windshield.

"This bend coming up scares the daylights out of me, especially since that godawful accident last spring."

The bend on Hulmeville Road is such that the average driver must slow to twenty. They had recently erected a concrete barrier because a man had tried to take it fast. He ran himself and his family into the half-frozen creek, leaving just a silver bumper jutting out with a sticker that said millions had died in machine-gun deaths. The Daily Trentonian had printed a half-page photograph of the car just as it was fished from the water by a tow-line, showing four lifeless bodies behind the icy windows and the detail was clear enough to reveal their white corneas: terror had come to their eyes in their final moments beneath the surface.

Edgar had hung the picture on his refrigerator, commenting to Skipper, "It's a terrible shame but let's face it, the idiot couldn't negotiate the curve and that's one hell of a picture besides." For a time, Edgar had slowed down a bit going around that bend and looked out to the river and wondered what it was like to plunge into an ice-cold river with wife and sons. He was convinced it could never happen to him. He knew the curve too well and now, at worst, the cement wall would stop his drowning. Besides that, he had no wife and no sons. He often pondered what was worse: going down to a watery death with loved ones or staying alive and alone.

An old white station-wagon slowed in front of him at the bend, and he crept up to notice the plate marked Disabled Veteran. The man behind the wheel had greasy black hair hanging from a bald spot. He cocked an eye into the rear-view mirror as Edgar closed in on him.

"What are you doing, you're getting too close," came the remark from his mother. "Are you trying to run that poor man off the road?"

"Well, the guy's cow-poking along. I can't go any slower."

"It's a dangerous curve for God's sakes, slow the hell down this instant, you're doing almost thirty."

"Thirty is slow, Ma, I hate to break the news to you."

"Tell that to the poor dead family they fished from the river. I'll bet that man said the same thing to his wife before he went in." She stopped and sighed loud and shook her head and fixed her collar. "Think of me at least Edgar if you're not going to think of yourself. I might be old but I still want to die respectable."

Edgar slowed to a crawl as the white station-wagon pulled ahead. The needle dropped to fifteen, and it was as if a cramp has settled in his right leg as he gently tried to rest it atop the gas pedal and keep the needle pegged where it was. The torturous tingle went up his side then through his fingers, touching the wheel and tightening his jaw . The white car had only five yards on him.

"This is ridiculous," he said.

"This is safe," she said.

The curve was behind him. Now, the road opened up as Edgar anticipated gunning the car up to a better speed. This is the stretch where, as a teenager, he would tear along with Danny in his GTO, racing him up to the Fonthill light at a hundred or so. Nostalgically, he would always push the pedal to the floor just as the curve ended and get the adrenaline pumping through his bloodstream on this straightaway as he shot to the light, and it would make him remember Danny and his laugh. But the white car would not oblige him as it crawled along at thirty and suddenly he felt his unconscious desire to floor it ripped away. This was suffocation, he thought, like that family in his picture on the refrigerator, sunk down below the sunlight with nothing left to breathe. It had come to him just then, the revelation of what had possessed him to hang the photograph: it was the way his mother had made him feel.

"I know what you're thinking," she said. "Don't you dare pass him... you've got a double yellow and they can revoke your license for passing on double yellow and you know it."

She looked over at him and behind the glasses and beneath the folds of skin and all around the old bones he could see the woman that stood on the step twenty-five years earlier, lingering there as he pumped his legs and got the swing higher, calling for him to come down because he was much too high. He was fighting just to get into the trees, he just wanted to be able to reach out and grab some maple leaves from one of the top branches. His little fingers were so close, but alas the pumping of his legs gave way to her demand, robbed the fury from his mission. The inevitable pull of gravity brought him down to the dirt.

"Ma, I really wish you would get off my back...listen to yourself, just listen. Cause I've had to listen all my goddamn life." Edgar looked ahead as the man in the white car ran fingers through his hair and cast another eye to his mirror as the cars got close.

"I'll bet if I made a little recording of your bitching," he said, "just a half-hour tape and had you listen to it every day for twenty years, after all that time you'd be tired of it, very tired of it. You wouldn't like yourself very much."

Edgar wished he hadn't said what he said and felt the thick wall of silence his mother was building in the middle of the seat. His only hope was a subject change.

"I wonder what war this guy was in," he said, pointing ahead. "See the plates. Ma? Veteran, it says." Pass him, Edgar thought. No cars were coming, and his needle sat on thirty. Years back, he would have shot past the guy and glared at him as he floored it. Skipper would have yelled something from the passenger seat over the roar of the engine. They'd be sitting at the light twelve miles up by now with empty beers, waiting for the red to change.

It suddenly hit Edgar that the road was double yellow all the way, and he had gone and sentenced himself behind both a slow driver and his mother's wall of silence. He calculated it might take an extra half-hour to get to Aunt Rita's.

"I hear Aunt Rita's operation went O.K," he said.

"Hmm" came a hopeful reply.

"I hear she wanted to save some ulcer samples in a plastic jar so she could send them to Uncle Frank and show him what he did to her insides."

Edgar glanced across at her stone frown and she turned her head away to look at the slow-moving trees, bothering a boat rider nearby with her Coke-bottle-eyed stare. The rider was a shirtless boy, no more than twelve years old. His paddles wavered the filmy surface, so the boat shifted direction.

"I'll bet this guy up here in the car was in Vietnam," Edgar said. "In fact, you know what, I'll bet he was a prisoner-of-war the way he drives so slow. Look at him, he's a mess... probably scared to death of gasoline."

Edgar imagined some dark cell where the man was strapped to the wall like Jesus to a cross, his head hung down just like Him, waiting in agony as the footsteps drew close; then the harsh glare of the light bulb would burn his eyes as the cell door opened. His captors would stand before him and babble with angry, foreign faces contorted in the dim light, bringing out pins and rods from the darkness to inflict pain. The man probably didn't understand a word of their language, nor did they of his. They wanted information, yet there was no way he could give it and no way for them to receive it. His only choice was to bear the torture as they raised the metal rods up to his face in angry gestures, finally plunging them into various spots on his body.

Edgar stared at the eye looking back at him from the rear-view mirror: he could imagine it ten times wider, as fear and pain descended in excruciating bursts. He could hear the wails of despair echoing out of his cell, pleading for them to stop. Hopeless screams, he thought.

Eventually, the man was let go, but only after they had effectively mangled his legs and castrated him with wire. He probably was dragged in a coma to a helicopter and recovered in some overcrowded hospital with no loved ones to visit, then given a little torture reimbursement check after he'd been wheeled out, out of which he went and rented a roach-filled apartment and bought a car. But now the money had all run dry and the car had one hundred fifty thousand miles on it and was burning a quart of oil a day and had begun to rot out in the floor and maybe he didn't want to drive past thirty because he was afraid of anything that had a chance of causing physical pain or maybe it was just because the car couldn't get up that high any more.

His mother sneezed and Edgar watched her as she sifted through her purse for a hankie. The snot sat on her lip.

"God bless, Ma," he said, with no reply.

His mother's death loomed on the horizon, and with that death he knew would come his remorse for never having gotten along with her, never being able to smile and laugh like most mothers and sons and somewhere there was an answer and a happy ending but all he could find was more hate and despair as the days and years piled up . He was faced with the most cumbersome paradox of welcoming her death to end all of the friction yet fearing the canyon of emptiness that would take its place.

The cramp left his leg. So, too, did the tingling that had reached to his fingers and had swam about his ears. He was doing thirty and it was no big deal now. The white car pulled off to the side of the road, where Edgar noticed some ducks climbing up the embankment near a picnic table shrouded in tall weeds. The man had some slices of bread, no doubt, and he was going to hobble on his crutches to the bench, brush aside the tall weeds, and feed the ducks. He'd probably sit and talk to them and break off little pieces and tell them about all of the tortures men did to other men and how he didn't know how much longer he could go on with his mangled legs and his dark memories and the ducks would never understand any of this because they were just there for the bread.

Patches of sunlight moved across the empty road as the clouds drifted by above the treetops. The wall of silence was fortified now, and it might be a week or so before it would be torn down. Edgar's foot did not respond to instinct this time, as the speedometer barely climbed above thirty. What was the point of racing to Aunt Rita's anyway, she was just going to get on him about finding a girl and getting a family going before it was too late and by the time he left he'd feel all empty and alone and then he'd give Sammy a call and they'd go over to Small Fries and get drunk again so he could numb his dark thoughts.

Edgar could see a car gaining quickly on him in his mirror. In seconds, he calculated, it would be on his tail and this one might put the lights on. Soon, he would be able to see the profanities spilling from the man's mouth as his jaw tightened. Edgar felt a slight dizziness swarm the inside of his skull and the hazy numbness of a dentist's chair descended. It felt different to drive slowly, a rather pleasant feeling of controlling someone else. He had this guy in his power: he could see the man was hesitant to pass him, so Edgar decided he would keep on going slow just to make him loosen his tie. Pass me, go ahead and pass me, Edgar was daring him. But you're going to have to break the law and cross double yellow.

Edgar looked at the two yellow lines dividing the lanes and watched as his mother craned her head to look back, knowing that at any moment she was going to tell him to stop it right now and get up to a reasonable speed. She was going to tug at her belt and snap it back, so it bolted her in tighter. Edgar glanced at his segmented reflection in the rear-view mirror, to see whether there was any kind of smudge on his face and noticed he had a bit of a smile.

AUGUST 4, 1966: Kids Stung by Bees
While Their Mothers Think They Are Dancing
and Singing Songs from "Those Damned Beatles"

JO-JO WAS STUNG seventeen times and had to go to the hospital, but not before his mother, and all of the other mothers in the Luft yard, including mom, thought he was clearly the best dancer of us all. That infernal screaming, that damned rock and roll, was another matter, however. It was just bad music and not good for anyone. Thinking we were all screaming that *Help* song they had heard on the radio over and over, they went back to their business of tea and gossip until the truth arrived writhing at their feet.

MY MOTHER PUT me in a baking soda bath to heal my stings, and she apologized for not knowing right away about the bees—at the same time knowing, the way a mother knows, that the bee stings would go away, but the Beatles would not.

BUBBLES

ON SATURDAY MORNINGS Penny the surprise lady came to the playground in front of the swings in a station wagon filled with crafts. She would park beneath a heavy tree, sit along the edge of the sandbox, and wait almost an hour for the sun to blaze through the leaves. I arrived by nine, along with a stream of kids from five to twelve years old, kids filtering down from Newportville Road and Hazel Avenue and Vandegriff Lane by way of the green bridge. Nine o'clock was what Penny waited for, and at five past nine she would get up from her spot on the wood, unhitch the gate of her wagon, and slide out boxes of construction paper and scissors and tin sheets into which we would hammer patterns of frogs and vicious dinosaurs and trees bearing large round fruits. And then we would play sloppy games of baseball or freeze tag or go on long scavenger hunts searching for things deep in our mothers' dresser drawers and at the bottoms of boxes in our basements, and we would always come back with our paper bags filled, and we would always give Penny reasons to smile.

Of all the things out of the back of her wagon though, Penny's bubbles still return to me in my sleep, forty-five years later. It is as if someone breathes into my subconscious and releases them, some phantom that stands on the edge of something dark and deep, someone with a secret to keep. Like apparitions, the bubbles float through my dreams, always out of reach, rising and near invisible, relics from those mornings in the sun when patterns would be indelibly hammered. But bubbles also come back with dreams of my father as he is leaving in the middle of the night with a gentle closing of the door; they float over his hushed footsteps, down the gravel walk and into oblivion. Sometimes I am trapped in one of my bubbles—not floating or carefree like the bubbles out of Penny's magic wand. Instead, my dream bubbles are earthbound and thick as a windshield, and I find myself, more than wishing to escape, wishing simply to be free of the ground.

My father was laid off from his job as an astrophysicist during the week I turned two, and from that point on, he couldn't find anything remotely steady. They didn't need anybody to look at the stars where we had settled, mainly because they had to tear the observatory down on account of the bright lights coming out of the newly built subdivisions. He worked for a while at the Shop-Rite bagging groceries by day, but that left him angry and drunk by night. He cursed his way out of his job during an afternoon of long check-out lines by laying into a bad-mouthed manager and found himself drunk off beer and Scotch in the early morning hours as he stumbled through our door. He soured on all work after that, and it took him months to even venture near a Help Wanted section of the *Evening Bulletin*. He never worked two straight months again, and he could never get himself to look skyward.

My mother told me stories of the house we once lived in before my memory, a bi-level green house in Fergusonville, set back on a quarter mile of cut grass. The house blended like foliage into a backdrop of lush woods and in her memory she could still smell the cedar of its sturdy walls; she could still feel the deep splinters in the tips of her fingers from lifting heavy windows and letting in the spring air; she could still hear the happy sounds as I called out, for more milk or a lost crayon perhaps, from the freshly painted nursery. Back when we had money, she said. Back when my father, filled with facial hair and the promises of a long career discovering constellations, kissed her and held her on clean sheets and a queen-sized bed, she said. Back when the world was a happy blue, she said.

As long as I can remember, though, we were piss poor, living in a two-room shack at the dead end of Hazel Avenue and subsisting on the handouts of Mrs. Butterworth and the Helmuth family. Canned goods mostly, assorted soups and creamed corn and sometimes gravies which we would pour over bread and fashion as our dinner. On lucky days, Mrs. Butterworth would bring McDonald's food for us, and the smell of hamburgers and French fries would settle into the shack for a good three days afterward. I believe we survived many nights by lingering smell alone, as my mother, in her careful acts of conservation, waited for just the desperate moment before she would take the can opener to the soups.

Never in all her years did she mention my father leaving. She never cried or carried on, never took to alcohol or God. All she did was go on, trying to make me presentable for St. Thomas Aquinas School in my soiled shirts and fitting newspaper snugly into the bottoms of my rotting shoes. She would take tiger lilies and honeysuckle from the roadsides and rub me with the fragrances before I went off because she didn't want me wallowing in shame in the back row, and because the flowery smells reminded her of the soap she used to be able to buy when the world was a happy blue.

One morning on the stoop, I heard my mother telling Mrs. Butterworth that she didn't blame my father for leaving. That if she were a man and the head of a household, well, she might have done the same thing. Terrible to be without a job for so long, she said, with so many millions of stars yet to be catalogued. Terrible to be hopeless and so justly angry at the world, she said. Terrible to be terrible at everything but gazing through a telescope, she said.

WE WAITED ALONG the edge of the sandbox for almost two hours on the morning that Penny stopped coming. The day had started gray with a threat of rain, and in those ticking moments, moving the sand into mountains with our feet, we simply figured that Penny had seen the sky and stayed home. We wondered where she came from, why she had just shown up in her wagon beneath the tree one morning, and then every Saturday morning of the summer thereafter. Never had I seen so many of us congregated in one place, so many kids excited about the long, fruitful day about to unfold because of one loving, caring woman. Penny expected us, too, all of us from Newportville and Hazel and Vandegriff, just as she opened the magnet of her magical gate. She gave us the games and creations to fill our days, and I'm sure all of us, each in our beds at night, silently asked the same things: what makes you do all of this for us, lady? Who are you, anyway? I thought perhaps that she had arrived in her wagon from the stars, because when I looked at the sky at night, I thought not of my father but of Penny and the coming day.

Saturdays emptied. Penny never came back, and as the weather turned cold, the kids, like animals drawn into hibernation, buried themselves away. They disappeared back across the green bridge, back down those long tree-lined roads, now hidden behind living room curtains in front of television sets or under earphones filled with loud guitar solos, or finally in the back seats of smoky automobiles and scattered like spores on the wind, never to return.

I THINK THAT my father is still alive somewhere out on the coast. I don't know why I think of the coast, perhaps from all the little bits of conversation I recall from my mother so long ago. The coast would seem to fit him best, in some dark mountainous space where he could finally ruminate on his own sky. He must be in his late seventies by now, his face battered by the sea to well over a hundred, his spirit long since submerged in the depths of suffering and alcohol and a longing for the family he left behind, the suns too late to discover.

Sometimes I think about meeting him on his death bed surrounded by many glowing candles-and what I might say. My mother, dead now almost ten years, would have liked to have seen him dying, too. She might have been angry for the first few seconds, but the anger wouldn't have lasted, I know that. She would have crumpled to the ground in pity, taken his aged hand and passed her forgiveness through to him and told him that the world was a cruel place for ones like him, ones who just couldn't find the proper road. Go on and die in peace, she might have said. And I might have lit another candle and whispered much the same thing.

I'm at the bottom of my bottle now. I can begin to taste the backwash and the liquid no longer burns my throat. A stiff breeze has come up, and I'll need to find a place where the wind doesn't come barreling down the brick quite so harshly. Maybe over on Midvale, maybe down one of the stairwells of those doctors' offices inhabited only by day. I can retire easily there. I can sleep a few hours there before the light comes back.

Whiskey always makes me dream. Some of the hard stuff, like that Jameson's I put down four nights ago, gives me terrible dreams where I wind up pissing my pants. There's nothing worse than waking to cold wet urine all down your legs, with the certainty that the smell will rise as the sun bakes you dry. People don't like it when you stink like that. I think I'll keep off the whiskey for a while, at least if I can help it. But I'll dream tonight, no doubt about that. I've thought long and hard about my past again, and with nearly a bottle in me, that's a sure sign that some dreams will visit.

If I could put something certain in my mind just as I drift off, then maybe I could break out of my bubble this time, crack right through it with several angry jabs of my fists. I could kick and scream and will myself free, burst that blasted bubble into a million molecules of soapy water. Or I could spread myself thinner and thinner across its transparent walls so that I would float clear off the ground. Up over the walk, hovering over that beautiful green house in the woods, absorbed by the sound of crickets and by my mother's happy song seeping through the screens as she waits for my father to come home from a long day's work. I've seen bubbles hover like that, the ones out of Penny's wand. The air catches them from opposite directions as they hang transfixed upon the pull of the world, tumbling over and over, reflecting ground and sky, ground and sky, but not going anywhere at all. They hang silently in the trees, magically hushing the birds, magically hushing the children far below, children like me who wait for a sudden burst of wind to push them onward, upward, into the happy blue, and perhaps to find some undiscovered star.

THE RING CLOSET

THE CLOSET OF rings at the dental office of Dr. Richard Corn is only six inches wide. It has a customized little white door, a tiny brass knob, and ten perfectly crafted shelves. In that closet is a treasure of choice, a reward to pick out after enduring the pain of a filled cavity, the needles, and the smells of chiseled tooth. Dr. Corn has rings of every shape and sort, tiny little rings for girls, big fat rings with skulls and motorcycles for boys, ones with silver and blue shiny stones, and the ones on the top shelf, if you are tall enough, harboring red rubies and letters of the alphabet that will tell everyone in the world the beginning of your name.

I fell in love with Miriam Mackey in the second grade, and everyone says that was not love, silly, because second grade is way too early for love, but I was in love. During this time of certain love, I was eating Necco Wafers and broke one of my bottom teeth and had to get it fixed, so I had to pay a visit to Dr. Corn. More importantly, after the tooth was repaired, I was to visit the ring closet. From the third shelf, the girl's shelf, I chose a girl's ring. I passed up the skull ring (with blue stones for eyes!) on the fourth shelf for this one, the one silver and shimmering like love, the ring that housed ten tiny plastic diamonds, the one that would make her know second grade love.

I put the ring into my pocket, did not show anyone, and presented it to Miriam Mackey Monday morning as she was walking to her seat in the back of the first row. Addition and subtraction passed slowly that afternoon. After the numbers on the board were wiped away and class was over, I was still lost in the thought of missing a subtraction problem, so during the shuffle of everyone exiting, I didn't see Miriam Mackey leave. I was the last one out of the room in fact, and there, sitting on the top of the garbage pail, was the ring I had just given her. I wanted to pick it up and put it back in my pocket, but it was a girl's ring, and it was in the trash, and I didn't want to believe I saw it there, so I left it and tried to forget about it that day, and then day after day after day after that, and long after it had been dumped into the compactor, and then the incinerator in Lot B.

I saw Miriam Mackey come and go through classrooms and hallways until we went off to separate junior highs, never offering her so much as eye contact. As she grew older, she disappeared into a sea of students, where I might occasionally see, as heads bobbed in hallways, the light from the windows illuminate her blonde curls as she shuffled down, just like it did in that second-grade classroom with that second-grade light and feeding my second-grade heart as she made her way to the back row, only taller and taller now and not in any row at all.

It took me forever to fall in love again.

Don't' you remember Miriam Mackey? First row, second grade, back of the class? Blonde hair, curls, blue eyes? Don't you remember? I can't find her on Facebook, on Google, on anything cyber, in any old phone book, in anything anywhere. No one seems to remember her, not my sisters, not Davey, no Jo-Jo, no one. Like her leaving the classroom that day, she just vanished, whisked by fate somewhere into a world that no internet search will ever reveal.

I suppose now, when I think about her, I should imagine how things went for her over the years and contrast that with what might have happened had she kept that ring, hugged me after addition and subtraction, moved down the hall with me, past the doors, and into the bright world. Married me, had my sons, my daughters, sat finally in a rocker on a porch with me somewhere.

How shall I imagine her life now, the miserable life without me? Why didn't she keep the ring and at least throw it away later? Don't you know how I felt when I looked down into that trash can? You broke a second-grader's heart. We were destined to be together, Miriam, so why did you go ahead and ignore destiny? Your dead-end road is of your own making.

I married finally in my forties, and it is love, I must say, and to someone not blonde or blue-eyed at all. She will be delivering our first child sometime next month, so I am unsure why the memory of Miriam Mackey is coming back so strong in this moment as I lay here in bed and cannot sleep. Unrequited love in the second grade? That is what kept me awake, and that is actually quite silly if you think about it (as I have laying here in the night), silly to fall in love in the second grade. And taking half your life to get over this mythical love? Even sillier. So I imagine instead, because the light will soon be on the curtains, a Miriam Mackey with ten real diamonds clustered on her ring finger, happy with husband and lots of children, all of them sporting their mothers' curls and blue eyes, all of them with huge smiles, and none of them with cavities. No cavities. No Dr. Corn. No ring closet. No broken hearts. Now I can sleep.

IDIOT BOY

EDWARD FIZZLE WAS up to his waist in snow and searching for the tractor keys when he noticed a sizable chunk of ice fall from the gutter of the barn and strike one of his father's cows directly on the head. His father had just plowed the pasture, and the cow, whose skull had punctured from the sharp missile, wobbled in a shaky gait across a wide patch of ice. It turned and flashed the whites of it eyes at Edward, and, in a fatal squeal, it crashed sideways into the fence and slid like an upended ship to the frozen ground.

"Well I'll be as damned as anybody," Edward called out. He stopped his search for the tractor keys, ready to leap in several long hurdles out of the snowbank to help the poor fallen creature. Then he eyed the back door of the house: his father would be out to inspect the cow, and Edward had to have the keys or he would be beaten again with the belt and sent to the cold loft for another long night. He retraced his deep footprints to the barn, watching for a gleam of steel that might shine up and deliver him from another punishment. He had circled the barn several times, and now he stood and looked at the infinite trail of footprints circling round and round. "What in hell was I thinking?" he asked to the dead cow. "How could I be like I am?"

Edward looked up at the ice hanging from the barn's roof. He was certain that he had loosened some icicles up by stamping his feet into the snow as he tramped around the edges of the barn. "I warmed the earth and shook them up and killed that damned cow," he whispered in a frosty ball of air. He feared that his father would reason the same thing when he saw the idiotic circles, so he began to scoop handfuls of snow from a fresh bank to cover his footprints, working at such a frantic pace that he began to gasp for air. All the while he watched the back door as he shoveled new snow into his tracks. He continued until he reached the back of the barn.

In his reasoning, Edward didn't consider that the sun, which had begun to thaw the ice, had actually loosened the weapon from the gutter. His father would no doubt see water dripping from the ends of the icicles above him and, in his infinite unidiotic wisdom, know immediately what natural elements had conspired to kill his cow. In truth, he would never consider blaming his son for this one; there would be no reason at all to send him to the loft.

Edward had built a considerable coating of sweat in his frantic cover-up, which had soaked the clothes beneath his winter coat. He stopped to gather more winter air into his lungs. "Oh Holy Jesus," he suddenly exclaimed. "I've covered my tracks and now I'll never find those keys." His heart raced as the back door slammed, as his father plunged in deep leaps across the field. "Shelley, Shelley," he called. He made his way through the snow, then walked across the frozen pasture to the dead cow lying along the fence. He knelt before the still animal, ran his gloves along the already-cold hide, and turned back to look at Edward, who had just dropped his handfuls of snow.

"Icicle killed her," Edward called out. He pointed nervously to the barn roof. "Saw the whole thing. Came down like a rocket."

"Get over here you idiot," his father screamed. Edward retraced his last uncovered prints, his eyes down in one last search. He stepped across the plowed land, feeling as if he had ventured into a ring in which he would have to confront his father for some bogus championship. He looked to the farmhouse for his mother in the hopes that the match could be warded off by the smell of pot roast or something.

"You stood out here and let Shelley die?" His father got up from his knees and moved closer; Edward guarded his face with a nervous revolution of hands.

"Wasn't much I could do," he replied. "Snow was deep, thing came down like a rocket."

"Rocket schmocket." He whacked Edward across the back of his skull and dislodged his cap. "What were you doing out by the barn anyway? I thought I told you to get the drive plowed."

Now Edward envisioned the tractor, still covered in snow, parked along the fence just behind the barn. He was going to have to explain the lost keys now and prepare his bed in the loft for another cold night. He remembered the last time he had slept there, just three nights ago, when the wind whipped up a ferocious noise all through the rafters and sent him into a long fit of nightmares from which faceless men with pitchforks, fanged farm animals, and an army of monster fathers arose. Besides all that, his hands and feet, despite being buried in straw as he thrust about in his sleep, had nearly frozen. He could feel the fresh bandages covering his frostbite sores. The gauze slid along the perspiration beneath his gloves and filled the rims of his eyes with tears. His father raised a hand again as the icy wind whipped his exposed face. He stepped away from the carcass.

"Getting to it," Edward said. "It's just that the cow dying kind of scared me is all." He moved out of range of his father's slap and stepped back into the snow toward the other side of the barn. Now what? He searched in silent prayer for the miracle of the discovered keys, for a little hole in the snow into which he might plunge his hands and retrieve his benediction. He looked to the sky in hopes that Providence would arrive on a beam of light and the sound of a jingle. Then he realized the hopelessness of his search as he crunched through the virgin snow on his way to the parked tractor. He could feel his father's eyes watching him, the same way in which he could feel deer watching him through underbrush as he loaded his rifle on hunting trips. His father walked out to watch him circle the barn, start the tractor, and head on down to the foot of the drive to begin three hours of plowing. Turning, he caught his father's frosty breath along the fence, as he stood, frozen still like an undaunted deer, with hands on hips.

Edward jumped into the tractor seat and pretended to fumble for the keys in his coat. He gripped the wheel and slid down into the cold seat so that the encrusted snow soaked through his pants. He looked straight ahead, hoping that his father would tire of the cold and make a return to the warm kitchen, where he would inform Edward's mother of the dead animal and prepare to carve it up: he would need to get it out of there before it began to rot, peel the good meat away himself with one of the long blades from the barn.

"Come on, come on, go back inside," Edward willed to the air. Then he heard a door slam across the fields, and he hunched down into the seat, sighed a moment's relief, and slid his hand, out of habit, toward the empty ignition.

He wanted to go back inside himself; the aroma of a roast had taken to the air upon his father's opening of the door, and his stomach seemed to be pulling him from the seat toward the porch light which his mother had just flicked on. If she had the courage, she would no doubt have shouted out to him that dinner was ready and to never mind the unplowed driveway. If she had the courage she would have lectured his father, as Edward made his way eagerly through the snow, on the importance of a warm fire and a hot meal for their son, that a full stomach and a happy heart were more important things than a cleared driveway. With courage she would have sat his father down and told him their son could plow the driveway tomorrow if he could get up a little earlier, and then make sure that he had second and third helpings. She would have said all of that if she had the courage. At that, Edward might have had the courage to point out to the high drifts and say simply 'I lost the keys somewhere out there. It's just one of those things.' Then he'd watch as his mother warded off his father's tirade, and with maternal precision, affirm the importance of securing valuable things. And Edward would have assured the both of them, as he finished his hot meal, that it would not happen again.

The biting cold came up in a wall of wind and slammed into Edward's face with the force of one of his father's slaps. He wouldn't be able to sit in the seat like this for very long; he would need to think up an excuse before he made his way back to the house. No matter what he came up with, it wouldn't do. Fury would fill the house; shouts and slamming and cursing would shake the foundation. In the aftermath of slamming doors in which his mother would retire to her room, he would be sent across the field, with no light at all, to spend another long night in the barn. The frostbite sores glowed hot beneath his wet gloves and reminded him of his unpromising future.

The cold had come up suddenly, and he shivered both from the chill of the evening air and from the fear that he might not make it through the night this time. "This cold this early in the day means below zero for sure tonight," he said into the wind.

Out beyond the fence, where the road dipped into the snow-filled valley,

Edward gazed in an unbroken stare and formed a plan. It was not much of a plan really, more an alternative to what awaited him on his return to the house. He found, in the sudden drop of light, that he could no longer bear to slink to his father's chair and, with his head hung in shame, inform him of another misdeed. He could no longer stand in the awkward silence of seconds turned hours and await the back of his father's hand, delivered out of an explosion of rage followed by his unworthy punishment. One more time he would watch, out of his tearful eyes, as his mother made her way to the back of the house to shut her bedroom door. Mostly, though, he could not bear to be called "idiot boy" one more time. That, more than the sting of his father's slap or the frostbite descending on his extremities, was what he could no longer take. That word, 'idiot,' sank down into every fiber of his being like slow poison. 'Idiot' struck marrow and pushed him like a tack into the wall. All he wanted was to rise above that, to go on for a time without committing one single act of stupidity, or to not be reprimanded for some senseless act he might invariably commit. He wanted to simply be understood, to be called 'idiot boy' never again. But Edward knew that his father's anger would never cease, that his mother would never find the fortitude to open her door and step in. So he gazed long and hard into the valley with its snow and its wind, and he decided he would rather go down there instead.

When the sun dipped behind the branches, the temperature plummeted ten degrees and set the sky to a metallic blue, much like the color of his father's truck. Just as Edward slid off the tractor seat and made his way in heavy footsteps through the snow beyond the fence, he could feel the icy air dropping like water inside his clothes. He wished he could go back to the house for a new pair of dry gloves and a scarf, so he could warm himself by the stove and get the chill out before he went off. He hurried his footsteps away from the property, however. Without the sound of the tractor cutting through the air, his father would be out at any moment with his rage and his punishment.

Edward, in his haste, tumbled down the hill on the other side of the road. His feet kicked up the powder and his heel caught on a buried boulder, sending him in a roll to the bottom some forty feet below. And then he was on his feet again and running as fast as he could through the deep snow, for he thought he had heard the slam of the back door, and he knew he needed to run: if his father caught him covered in snow at the bottom of the hill, on the other side of the fence, off the property and in the valley, he would surely beat him into a black-and-blue pulp. That, together with the lost keys, and the lingering thought of one of his best cows dead, would be too much. So Edward kept running and he pumped his legs through the deep snow until he finally fell in a heap several hundred yards into the valley.

He had to gather his breath and think about his next move, so he sat, with many huge question marks, upon a snow-covered log. He was far enough away from the house so that he did not fear his father's sudden appearance out of nowhere, and he welcomed the moment's relief. In his delirium of sudden change, a fog of futures rolled across his brain in a rapid drift, never stopping to solidify anything concrete. Instead, he beheld only a glimpse of hopeful summer lawns and rooms full of love —somewhere, he guessed, in a strange house, on the other side of the valley. Some smiles, some meals prepared with care, some freshly washed sheets into which he could peacefully dream. On the other side of the valley, in another season, absent of mistake.

He listened for a sound and considered the many times that his father had appeared out of nowhere. When Edward had overflowed the toilet, he had turned and found his father there in the bathroom doorway, appearing without a sound, phantom-like, his hand already raised. At the dinner table one evening, Edward had filled his pockets with his mother's burned steak, and was caught, as if by magic, emptying them below the coffee grounds in a garbage pail. Even at two years old, just after he had finished a doodle in red crayon on the nursery room wall, his father had walked in on air and slapped him clear across the room, sending the crayon into a spray of crumbled wax across the floor. As the images froze like broken icicles, the haunting presence of his father became so thick, even in the valley, even half a mile away, that it got Edward's legs moving after he caught only a few breaths.

Fear made him forget about his cold body, which had begun, slowly and unknowingly, to succumb to the elements. It was not long — perhaps two miles into his journey to nowhere through the dead underbrush — that Edward lost the feeling in his legs and hands. His head swam in a warm sea of fear, bobbing in disillusion to the sound of a slamming door miles away, to the crunch of snow on a hilltop unseen, to the advancing footsteps over boulders and logs toward his running form, phantom footsteps impaled upon the dead valley. The ghost advanced, quicker than the wind, quicker than a thousand painful memories and a thousand needles of pain through his bandaged hands. "He is coming... I had better keep moving," he willed to the black valley air. "I cannot stop for a very long time."

Somewhere out past Abigail's farm Edward fell. A large toppled tree had risen suddenly out of the snow-covered valley like a monolith. Its large dead stumps, under the pale moon, looked much like the raised arms of his father, exaggerated and gnarled as they twisted in an organic descent toward his shivering body. In a moment of panic, he attempted to leap the monstrosity, but his numbed legs could not carry him up and over. Fully upended, his feet slid along the thick snow-covered bark and sent his head spinning into a web of branches, where he fell into a long, dreamy daze.

He laughed finally; he had been lying motionless in the snow for nearly ten minutes, but finally he laughed. "You're not my wicked horrible father," he shouted. "You're nothing but a dead, stupid tree, and I'm stupid for not noticing that you're a dead, stupid tree." He sighed and watched his frosty breath rise toward the moon. "I'm afraid of nothing. You hear that you dead, stupid tree? I'm afraid of nothing."

Edward tried to get up. He had every intention of making his way back across the valley, back across his frantic tracks, back up the hill and across the road, past the blasted tractor and over the dark fields. He was going to burst through that back door. He was going to warm his fingers and then tell his father he was tired of being an idiot. He was going to tell his father to stop all the shit and just plain let him live, that no human being deserved his sort of treatment. He would order his mother to his side and, with her arms draped around him, she would finally come out and tell her husband much the same thing. "Leave our poor boy be —

he's trying very hard to just be." Edward had the whole scene, in one moment of enormous clarity, perfectly mapped out. But he could not move his legs, and an incredible warmth began to seep through his toes as he turned his eyes to the moon and back again.

Then he laughed again—not at the father-like tree which had upended him, nor at the crystal vision of confronting his father as it deteriorated to ridiculous fantasy—but at the gleaming metal he beheld, just at the edge of his trouser waist, in the failing moonlight. "The keys," he said. "They must have slipped down into my pants somehow. I must have shaken them out when I fell." In frantic delight, he tried to maneuver his hands downward to snatch the keys and close his fingers around them. But the cold biting air had numbed his extremities to uselessness. After a long struggle during which he exerted every ounce of thawed muscle to reach those keys, his arms finally fell limp along the bark of the cold, dead tree. Edward smiled in warm surrender. "I am not the idiot that I thought," he said in an assured whisper to the invisible ghost he was quite sure hovered within earshot. "A hole in my pocket...a freaky thing that could have happened to anyone. The important thing is, I didn't lose them." Now he considered that perhaps he was no idiot all along, and that it was only bad luck which had plagued him the whole of his life, that a backed-up toilet and a burned steak and long streaks of crayon across the nursery walls could have happened to just about anyone. All along, he thought in a frosty ball, all he needed was a pocket without a hole. Just a lousy stinking pocket without a hole. He laid back and watched the moon become swallowed by clouds. He wished he could have gotten up to start that tractor, to fill the night with sound, to plow hard into a wall of snow and forever drown out his father's shouts. Yes, clear the drive of snow and fill the night with sound: that was his only wish now. That was all he wanted as he drifted into his warm sleep.

SECRET STITCHES

On the evening of the day that Amy turned seven, her brother Paul, after watching an episode of "Mannix", tied her up and made her walk across the hard tiles of the kitchen floor until she fell directly on her face. Their father Alex, down between the pages of the Daily News, heard the thud and the cry and finally Paul's gasp as the blood flowed from the kitchen above, thinking only that the sounds resembled the sounds of any other scuffles that had erupted between the two over the course of years. He finished his paragraph and ruffled his paper, then stopped at the curious silence. He turned his eyes finally to the top of the stairs, where Paul flashed the terror of his act and beckoned his father, without a word, from his recliner.

Amy spent the better part of two years in and out of hospitals— first the general ones, then a string of specialized buildings filled with foreign doctors. Because Amy's tied hands were unable to break her fall, her forehead had hit full force upon the tiles. Paul would later sob, over and over in waiting rooms, that he had seen her head bounce three or four times before it finally came to rest in a pool of blood, before her last whimpers settled into unconsciousness. Likewise on several occasions, his father sobbed and apologized for belting his son there in the kitchen immediately after the medics had carted Amy away, after he had to explain the knotted ropes to the men who had to kneel and unravel Paul's scoutsmanship. Paul, questioned in a corner, had elaborated in whispers, with trembling limbs, about the particular episode of "Mannix" which had possessed him to fetch the rope from the basement and grab his little sister by the waist. "It just felt like the thing to do during the commercials," he had said as he stared into the wallpaper pattern.

Suffering amnesia, Amy couldn't remember much of anything except that she had just turned seven, and of a television advertisement, word by word, for Life cereal. At first she remembered her name as Mikey. However, upon seeing her reflection in a mirror, she understood that she was neither a boy nor a commercial and dropped into a blank gaze which her father tried valiantly to penetrate by injecting various memorable events of her life.

Amy's father admitted her to St. Vincent's Neurological Hospital shortly after her ninth birthday. Dr. Ardizone, fresh up from Venezuela, probed her eyes with a powerful pen light and knocked about her head with repeated taps of his fist. "Not much we can do about the human consciousness," he said in his thick accent. "It's a deep dark mystery, especially with such a blow." He surveyed the long winding scar that tapered to her left ear and ran his finger along the ridge as if he were reading braille.

"When will the stitches come out?" Amy asked suddenly. The outburst, from her head of empty pages, surprised both her father and the doctor, who clicked off his pen light in amazement.

"You know about your stitches?" he asked. "You know that your stitches came out almost two years ago?"

"Yes, but not those...stitches on the arm..." Amy fell back into her silence and reached into her well to identify from where she had extracted such a remark. Her eyes scanned the room.

"How do you remember arm stitches, honey?" her father asked. "How would you know such a thing?"

"I remember a time....I remember a time..." She could only utter that, for a wall had obviously dropped on her memory of the arm stitches and closed her off, once again, into her suffocating universe. Her father, hopeful that signs of recognition were returning and that perhaps she would leap into his arms crying 'daddy' at any moment, moved into dejection as her glassy eyes returned.

Dr. Ardizone pulled Alex into the hallway. "She is not remembering the stitches she had removed last year...she is remembering stitches from another time, I'm sure of it." he said. "Did she ever have arm stitches as a baby? Did she know anyone who had arm stitches?" The doctor could not contain his excitement, wild-eyed and curious to dig deeper into her mysterious outburst, certain that this unconscious revelation would fill another piece of the puzzle to which he had been working to assemble his entire adult life.

Alex could only rub his chin, tick back the years, and remember nothing. "Never a stitch, never a memory of a stitch," he told the doctor. "Up until Paul tied her up, she's never been hurt other than scrapes on the knee. Nobody's ever been hurt. Not Paul. Not me. Don't know why she remembers arm stitches."

"What about your wife?" the doctor asked. "Perhaps she..."

"The children don't know their mother," Alex snapped, almost in a shout. He turned to the wall, avoiding eye contact with the doctor. "She left when Amy was still in the crib, when Paul was four. She....she left...." Then he braced his head against the wall, and Dr. Ardizone could see the painful memories returning to this particular consciousness as he delivered more space and let them escape. The hallway filled with the echoes of distant nurses, but it might as well have emptied completely of sound, for the stifling silence between them only resurrected the mystery of the departed wife, as Alex's past ground its torment to the surface.

"Tell me if there's any change," he told the doctor without eye contact and then: "Paul will be expecting grilled cheeses for dinner." He walked off towards the elevators without a good-bye to Amy, who wouldn't have recognized her own father anyway.

Later that night, after Betty the night shift nurse had finished her romance novel, a faint drone seeped out of Room 432 and issued itself down the hall like a fog. Amy, whom Dr. Ardizone later explained must have been caught in a dream, kept repeating "lavender" over and over, recanting the word as if ensconced in religious ritual.

"It was very frightening at three in the morning with the lights turned low," Betty wrote in her report. "Seated at my station, I was getting a piece of her memory over and over for near two hours like some Chinese water torture."

Of course, Dr. Ardizone questioned Amy that next morning, and upon her father's arrival, took him aside and tried to dredge up a lavender memory.

Alex, awake most of the night attempting to recount any possible stitching experiences, quietly rubbed his eyes. "Nope," he sighed in frustration. "Lavender doesn't bring back anything save for the lilac bushes in May."

The doctor considered a question involving the departed wife, but quickly remembered the man's previous day with the wall. Ardizone was certain that stitches and lavender had some distant connection, perhaps tied to some accident of which Alex refused to recognize. He reminded himself, in some clipboard scribbles, to pursue the memory of the mother, after Alex had a few more sleepless nights and could perhaps make a more fertile connection.

"You know, some doctors, including myself, believe that returning memories occur chronologically," he said to Alex.

"So what you're saying is..." Alex raised his heavy eyelids and beckoned the doctor's explanation.

"I believe that she may be remembering things from very early on... perhaps from infancy."

"Funny, I was thinking about my earliest memory as I was lying awake last night, after you'd asked about my ex-wife leaving," he said. "I was trying to remember as far back as I could....a thunderstorm coming in off the playground when I was four while my mother called me home from the back steps. The picket fence, so endless along the Luff's back yard....the lightning." He stopped and sighed, then gazed in anger at the doctor. "I was four, damnit. I can't possibly see how Amy could remember something from the crib."

"The dark well of the unconscious is sometimes clouded over by layers of memory. The older we get, the more difficult it becomes to remember things from long ago." Dr. Ardizone had planned to go on, to explain all about absence of language and how Amy's blank pages had taken her back to that time when the world filled itself only with unfamiliar shapes and sounds, to a place where no words encroached. In his own mind, things had begun to click into place—her view from the crib and what might have made her translate things into stitches: some intersecting lines, perhaps from a spinning mobile, patterned like the stitches running across her own head. And lavender: maybe it was the color of the walls, or a heavy blanket draped about her, or some sort of toy to which her eyes first focused. Perhaps she had marked up the wooden crib with a lavender crayon or had seen the lavender curtains moving on a gust of wind. He was going to go on and theorize all this aloud, but Alex had begun heavy sighs of anger, so he simply made himself some quick notes.

Later that night beneath his desk lamp, Ardizone penned comments into his journal which drew conclusions about Alex's missing wife: in one entry, she had left with a lover, and the sight of the man had elicited rage from Alex and then some deep cuts that required stitching. In another entry, a lavender vase was tossed across the room, smashed into jagged fragments all about the crib. Then others: Amy was cut and stitched somewhere else early on, and Alex didn't want him to know because his temper and child abuse would be dredged up; Alex had murdered his wife and wrapped her body in a lavender tablecloth and dragged her into the yard as Amy, in her wordless world, looked on. These things would be looked into, Ardizone promised himself in writing. He would get to the bottom of her consciousness and begin to solve the mystery of the human brain. Symposiums, lectures, book tours, talk shows, he kept thinking as he shut off his light and listened to the rain.

All along, back to when she first was admitted to West County General, Paul wanted to speak to Amy alone in her hospital room and apologize for what he had done. He could not shake the image of her falling; he could not fall to sleep most nights because her head kept bouncing off the floor and pestering him. It was there, spreading like a cancer month by month. He knew he needed to speak to her alone, despite her not knowing him as brother. Trying to work up courage, he had thought of asking his father several times to leave her hospital rooms so that he could be alone with his little sister. Paul could never get the words to the surface; he was afraid of the monster that Amy had become. Often when visiting, he would stand at the far end of the room, beneath the mounted television, while his father tried to get through to Amy. He would eye him as he repeated detailed memories or tickled her on the toes the way he had done since she was two or rubbed her stitches to see if something monumental would return. This was not the sister Paul once teased, the one whom he had walled into the snow fort, whose slippers he had filled with shaving cream. He had taken some things from her room one Christmas and wrapped them all and placed each of them with red bows in a pile beneath the tree. He had to hold back the laughter as she plunged gleefully into the pile and opened them one by one. Their father sat puzzled and finally began to snicker himself. "Hey I already have one of these," she kept saying as she opened each one. When her revelation, and then her anger, and finally some hollow laughter came out from her spot there on the rug, Paul whipped out his real present and slid it across. That was the other Amy, and every time he dredged up the pleasant memories, it became all that more impossible to imagine some time alone with what she had become. But he needed to do it——most of her life had been wiped away, and he needed to let her know that he had made it happen and that he was so sorry about it all.

The colors on the television flicked in and out in a heavy magenta and it irritated Paul. Flesh tones would only hold for several seconds before they would give way: it was like an itch coming on, yet despite all of the finagling of the antenna and the turning of the Hue and Tone knobs, the itch persisted. He shut off the set in frustration and waited for the sound of his father's car. Visiting hours had ended, and he would be driving down Mill Road with a load on his mind again. He was hoping his father would make spaghetti tonight. That was the only meal he could make right. He could still taste the burned grilled cheeses from last night's dinner.

Just after nine, the headlights came through the curtains and flooded the family portrait. Like every other night, Paul was hoping for some good news, perhaps even the sound of two car doors slamming and a fully recovered Amy bursting into the room shouting, "Paul Paul Paul." Only the one door: his father came quiet and perturbed into the room and dropped into his recliner, staring hard again at the paneling.

"Nothing again dad?" Paul asked. "No new memories?"

"As a matter of fact," his father replied "She came up with something out of the blue again. She's got a friend now, a black woman named

Peggy." He returned his stare to the paneling and sighed: "A black woman named Peggy."

Paul sank back into the couch and thought for some seconds. "Maybe a teacher? Isn't there a black woman up on Pelham named Peggy?"

"That's April and she didn't know April. It's not April."

Something familiar was brushing at the edge of Paul's brain, touching the tips of his memory cells like a feather. Peggy, a black woman. It almost came to him, then faded entirely. Had he met this woman? Had they met her together? Perhaps on one of the days they had walked down to the pond, someone had stopped and spoken. He vaguely remembered something. Then Paul tried to remember his mother. Was she black? He dare not ask his father. He checked his white arms.

"Why do you have the set off?" his father asked.

"Colors were giving me a headache."

"Put it on black and white then. That's what I do. Only way to watch it anyway."

Black and white, he kept thinking as he clicked "Beverly Hillbillies" back on. He turned both knobs left until the colors faded, then sank back into the couch, adjusted the pillows, and took in the canned laughter. Where is my mother anyway, he kept thinking as he watched Ellie May by the pool.

In one theory, Ardizone had a Black woman named Peggy, in a lavender dress, getting her stitches removed in an examination room. Alex, who had brought Amy to the doctor for her six-month check-up, mistakenly walked into the wrong examination room, quickly apologized, and closed the door. Not, however, before the fluorescent image of the black women, with her lavender dress and exposed stitches, had fully burned into Amy's memory cells. Ardizone commented, in parenthesis, that Alex would not remember such an event, so he was going to confront Amy about it instead.

Just after her breakfast, Ardizone entered Room 432 with his clipboard and got down to business. He had the memory all laid out and began forging questions in the hope that everything would come tumbling back. He knew that all it took sometimes was one word. One word, like a key, would unlock everything, and the memories would come flooding back. Amy, however, simply ran her fingers through her hair and shook her head. "Confused," she said. "Every day you come in here with things that I'm supposed to know and I feel dizzy every time you leave."

The doctor, so certain that he would elicit a spark with this theory, patted her on the back in subtle dejection. "That's a common side effect to amnesia," he sighed. "Much like thinking of food on an empty stomach. You're thinking memories on an empty brain."

"I do remember part of a dream last night though," Amy said.

The doctor readied his pen and moved close.

"I was tied up."

"You know that's how you fell. How you hurt your head."

"Yes, I know but this time I was in a chair, and there was a bad man, or maybe two bad men, but I couldn't see him or them. I think he or they left me alone in the house. I think he or they left in a car or something." Amy watched the doctors furrowing eyebrows as he wrote everything down.

"I tried to get up. I needed to get out of that room because something bad was going to happen. I got up from the chair. I saw the door, the door-knob. I...." She stared at the sunlight.

"Go on Amy. Try to remember."

"I think I fell."

"No one made you walk in your dream. No one was there with you?"

"No, I'm sure I was alone. I wanted to get to that door, and I tried to go too fast. My feet were tied. I fell."

Satisfied for the time and filled with a thousand theories, Ardizone moved quickly out of the room and down the hall toward his office. His mind raced: murder, kidnapping, evil doings. Amy had witnessed something, that was for sure. Perhaps she would reveal some deep dark secrets that Alex had made sure to cover over. She had witnessed it all from her crib, or crawled into the hallway while her father had his wife bound and gagged in the middle of the living room. She had watched as her mother made a frantic attempt at the door, only to fall, just as she had done when her own brother pushed her to the tiles. Perhaps she needed stitches beneath her lavender dress. Perhaps her father had married a black woman and had second thoughts, and he later found the time to stuff her in a trunk. Or perhaps her father was tied to that chair, and some masked men had taken her mother away. They had come for jewels and money, certain that her father had some to spare in one of the dresser drawers. When they found nothing, they took her mother away instead. She kicked and screamed, and her father tried valiantly to get out of the chair and get to the door. His face required stitches, and the police never found his wife.

Ardizone decided he wasn't going to run these particular theories by Alex: they posed problems with their seriousness and might cause the man to lose all control. Instead, he would check some incident reports down at the police station to verify any possible crimes. "Wouldn't that be something," he thought, "if I solved this puzzle, put together a better understanding of the human mind, and, at the same time, brought some criminals to justice?"

Alex arrived during afternoon visiting hours just after he had picked up Paul from school. As usual, Paul stood in the far corner as his father hugged and kissed Amy and tried to get her to remember her first seven years. He spoke in whispers, in the way that doctors in every hospital to which she had been admitted over the past two years had instructed him to do. The intimacy of the soft-spoken word might bring it all back, they had all told him. She might remember that same voice from a bedtime story.

Paul looked away, first out to the sunlight coming off the roof of the atrium, then out into the hallway, where the lunch cart lady was gathering discarded trays of half-eaten sandwiches and such. He wouldn't need to be here quite as long today—they had hit some heavy traffic on the interstate on the way over and visiting hours were nearly gone. Soon, in twenty minutes or so, it would be time to leave and go back home, where he could sink back down into the couch and watch his television.

Ardizone came into the room with his clipboard filled with notes and his eyes filled with fire. "Well look who came to visit you again today," he said loudly to Amy. "Looks like somebody loves you an awful lot."

Alex smiled and stroked her hair.

Ardizone had just come from the police station, where, after poring over thick piles of reports for three hours, he had turned up nothing that could support any of his theories. He was, however, resolved to finding an answer—in fact, more now than ever. The case history of Amy Stidum would enable him to put it all together, to write his book and take his place among the elite of the field. So certain was he that the fragments had a connection. Anger or no anger, he was going to extract something from Alex today.

"We need to talk in the hall," he whispered. Alex followed him toward the doorway. Paul's heart began to race, for he realized that he would be alone in the room with Amy for the very first time since the accident. This was the moment he could not work up the courage to ask for, and now, the doctor was handing it to him.

"Make sure she doesn't escape," Alex said into Paul's ear. Then they were gone.

"How goes it Amy," Paul said. The awkward moment consumed him, and he wanted to open one of her hospital windows, drop to the atrium, and escape himself. He wished for a nurse, someone to usher him from the room because visiting hours were nearly done. He checked the hall for a white dress and stuffed his hands into his pockets. He looked back to Amy.

"I always get these little headaches," she said. "I guess I should stop trying to think or something." She adjusted a pillow.

"Thinking hurts me too, especially the night before math tests," Paul replied. He was hoping for at least a smile for that one, but obviously Amy had no conception of math, or tests for that matter.

"Look Amy, I need to say this." He was doing it; he moved toward her bed, with no one else in the room, in the scenario that he had imagined for two years. He took her little hand and looked into her puzzled eyes. "I'm sorry I did what I did."

"Did what you did? I don't remember what you did."

"I know, but I'm sure you've heard. I tied you up and made you walk. I didn't do it to hurt you. I thought it would be funny to watch you walk and I'm so sorry. It's just that, well, on Mannix..."

Amy pulled her hand away, and the puzzled look in her eyes suddenly vanished. Paul stepped back, as if some beam of invisible light had shot down from the ceiling and enveloped his little sister on her bed. Her face muscles tensed, and her eyes grew wide.

"Paul," she said. "Paul."

"You...know me?"

"I know you...I know me, I know. Where is dad?"

Paul could not believe the transformation which had occurred right in front of him. What had he done? What had he said? She smiled in recognition.

Everything rushed back to Amy: first her name, resounding like a gong across her brain, then the memories, one by one, floating in like so much debris down a swollen river. The swings, the burned playground grass, the sandbox, the big rotted maple. The deep woods, the box turtles, the faces of boys running up the path— Joey Helmuth, Eddie Culp, Carl and then Paul in his muddy boots. The open windows, the garage filled with snakes, her room with the white vanity, the flower posters, the stained curtains. Her father pulling in the drive, the plastic seat so hot on summer afternoons, the smell of cigarettes lingering, Mill Road in the rain, the crickets so loud in August. I am Amy, he is Paul, I can hear my father out in the hallway shouting. I can write my name if I want, I can write 'Amy' if I want. And then Mannix: a man named Mr. Lavender, with stitches up his arm, tying Mike Mannix's Black secretary Peggy to the chair. Setting a bomb, leaving in a car, and then Peggy, wide-eyed and fearful, trying to escape. Hopping across the room, trying to make the door, reaching for the doorknob, falling, getting up, falling, getting to the door, getting out. A commercial, Life cereal, "I think I'll tie you up just like that" from Paul. Up to the kitchen, grabbed by the waist, the rope, the gag, the light overhead, the floor....

Paul rushed out of the room. He did not realize that he had found the magic word, that the word 'Mannix' had unlocked the door and sent her memories spilling out. His father, red-faced in anger, had backed Ardizone into a laundry cart. The doctor's clipboard had released its pages all over the floor and scattered notes about their shoes. It seemed to Paul as though his father were ready to punch the doctor, and he could see several wide-eyed nurses scurrying for help.

"Dad, dad, she can remember again, she can remember!" Paul shouted.

Immediately the doctor, then Paul and his father, rushed back into the room, where Amy, her memory intact, bolted from the bed and jumped into her father's arms. She told him about her spinning head, about the flood of memories still returning, about wanting to go home. "I'm me again, daddy," she said. "I don't need to be here more."

The doctor moved close and examined her as her father, still bristling from their altercation in the hall, picked her up and held her tight. Ardizone checked into her eyes with his penlight, tapped her head again with his fist, and stepped back while she kissed her father's cheek. Of course, he felt relief. She had fully recovered, and everything had come back to her, and that was always a good thing. But now his dream had died. He could no longer covet her case history and vault himself to stardom. All those scattered pages in the hall had become useless. He might still write a book, but it would not have the ending for which he had hoped. It would not have the flavor of an evil deed or a revelation that would jolt the medical world.

In all his theories, in all those long hours of note-taking, he had never considered the television; he knew nothing of 'Mannix' or any other American television shows for that matter. Had he known, had he theorized in that direction, he may very well have unlocked Amy's trapped memories himself. He may very well have written a best-selling book and visited talk shows and found his place among the medical immortals. Television and the Unconscious, he might have titled his book.

"How did she remember?" he asked Paul. "How did you make it all come back?"

For the first time since he had forced his tied-up sister to walk, Paul's posture straightened. A thousand needles had just been removed from his heart, and he hugged his father and sister and almost found the tears to cry. Stepping back from the embrace and standing proud, Paul turned to the doctor and said simply, "I apologized."

THE LOW SETTING

BACK FROM HIS hot drive along the squash fields and suspended beneath the warm air oscillating from the corner fan, Sal clipped his last toenail and flicked it behind the couch. He hummed a little burst of notes from a song which he couldn't remember the title to, a tune that reminded him of something his ex-wife out in Mayfair used to sing, when she was done up in the mornings in her curlers and burning up the muffins.

Sal could see out past the glare coming off the window box: the long shadow of a woman tapered around a cane and walking by, swaying and elongating like the thick shadow of a branch on the wall; swaying, stopping, swaying, moving close. Old Lady Crawford, he guessed, coming up the walk. Sal considered his two options again. He could sit silent while she ambled up and tapped on the windowpane and peered in on the room with her fogged eyes. Or he could just go to the door while she knocked, to listen to what he'd done wrong this time around. Old Lady Crawford would let him know loud and long about his cat sitting on her tomato plants to sun itself again, or Johnny cutting across her yard to the bus stop, or the rotted tailpipe that dragged with sparks from his car the last three nights he came home.

The stale air coming off the fan was buzzing on low. Sal began to feel the sweat forming on the back of his tee-shirt, and his temple began to itch, but he didn't feel like getting up off the couch to crank up the controls to medium or even to high. His ankles ached and besides that, he could see Old Lady Crawford's face behind the window box begonias, as she tapped her cane in several loud raps on the glass. She was trying to peek in for a look-see as she leaned over his short garden.

Sal stayed there on the couch, opting to sit silent. He closed his eyes, in case Old Lady Crawford could see that he wasn't sleeping, at which point she would begin to bay like a hound with that raspy voice of hers, commanding him to get up and answer the door, saying over and over to the neighborhood, "I know you're in there...I know you're in there."

Sal kept his eyes closed for a while, as he listened for the tapping of her cane and imagined her nose pressed against the glass, her eyes working behind those thick spectacles. But there was only silence outside his door. Sal figured she had given up without a fight this time and had gone away muttering to herself that next time she was going to shatter a window or have a police car waiting. She would go chasing after Johnny one morning with her cane and her anger, all the way to the bus stop.

The air coming off the fan began to feel invigorating on Sal's face as it oscillated over the beads of sweat. The weariness of his drive now began to consume him, as he felt the aching of his ankles begin to fade with the coming of sleep. Sal could still feel the burning sun of the squash fields and smell the hot vinyl of the car seat as he drifted into his dream of white hilly waves of sand. It was a world that rippled away forever, suddenly relaxing but still hot, as he walked alone in search of an ocean, deep and blue and cold. Then Sal was searching for Johnny in his dream. He was searching with a feverish importance, and a sudden fear had crept over him that they had become hopelessly separated by miles of desert, followed by the pervading fear that a sandstorm was approaching from somewhere out of an abyss. Sal followed Johnny's windblown footprints until they were faint scrapes on the sand, stretching out in all directions. The sun glowed like a flare, suspended perpetually above him, and he turned to look at his own footprints, noticing that they were gone, and he was buried to his knees.

Johnny jarred Sal awake in the darkened room. He stood over the chair, and Sal wasn't sure at first, but his immediate perception was of a monolith rising out of the desert, impaling itself upon his sunken form as he struggled to be free. Johnny's eyes flickered in a red light flashing through the window as Sal crawled to the shore of consciousness and recognized the room, the chairs, the fan. Glimmers of terror danced on Johnny's corneas, like the cat when it was confronted by a swinging two by four.

"They found her on the step, Pop. She doesn't look good."

Fully conscious and out of the chair, Sal moved to the window to see the ambulance, and a stretcher rolling into the back with a body, covered by a sheet. Sal could see the cane lying there on the walk. He tugged the curtain open more to reveal the sleek ambulance parked at an angle in the middle of the road and dark heads of neighbors moored against their porch lights.

A man brushed through the open door with tightened jaw and clipboard. "Mr. Taglio, you son John says you know this Elizabeth Crawford. Says she comes knocking sometimes."

"I know Old L...um, Elizabeth," Sal replied. "What happened out there?"

"Heart failure on your step, sir," said the tight-jawed man. "She died right there on your step."

Sal peeled away his sweat-soaked tee-shirt from his back. He looked again as they closed the ambulance door, as the man took his clipboard and scrawled his signature in the dark.

"Well, there's nothing more we can do here," he said.

"I was asleep the whole time," Sal said as the tight-jawed man walked out. "She must have been knocking for help and I was asleep the whole time. Those fans, you know, those fans, you put them on the high setting and they take away your hearing," Sal said, and then he noticed the slow-moving blades across the room, the near silence that pervaded his remark as the man moved an ear ever so slightly in the direction of the whirr. Sal remembered himself falling asleep hot and with his temple itching, thinking, "I'll just let it run on low."

Sal glanced at Johnny, and his eyes looked like the cat's eyes when it was given dry cat food. Johnny knew the whole routine, with the sitting quiet until she went away, and the little insults he and his father would whisper about "Old Lady Crawfish," and the way Sal had instructed him to go hide behind the checkered drapes. He'd taught Johnny how to be quiet and crawl across the carpet while she knocked. He taught him how to crawl with his ass down.

Now, Johnny knew that Sal had lied to the tight-jawed man. He knew Sal was awake the whole time. Old Lady Crawford was rapping on the glass because she was getting those terrible pains in her chest. The pains were so terrible that she wouldn't be able to make it home, so she had stopped to ask his pop's help. The pains were so terrible that she couldn't even call out. She could only swing her cane at the window. Johnny knew his pop had just sat there on the couch and played his game and listened to her die.

"Honest, Johnny, this time I really was asleep."

The tight-jawed man slid into the passenger side and shut his door, and then the driver pulled away and left the pulsating light to pass along the checkered drapes until it vanished red into the night. Sal turned to switch on the lamp, fumbling along the server and feeling the unblinking eyes of his son upon him in the darkness.

THE ABOVE

IT WAS THE day my brother turned twelve, in the year that I became nine, that Mike Schmidt hit a baseball so hard that our television imploded. At that age, you don't consider the mathematical improbabilities of two such events occurring at the same time, knowing full well that one had nothing to do with the other. If I had known, for instance, about television tubes burning hour upon hour in humid living rooms in the dead of August afternoons, that some part was bound to burn up sometime, and it would no doubt occur while the television was on—and all my father ever watched was sports, anyway—well then it wouldn't ever have become such a religious event for me. Schmidt, after all, hit home runs all the time; hell, any baseball game could have a handful of them by any number of other players. The raised volume level of Kalas's voice—"long drive, deep right field, watch that baby..."—well that could have been just enough to evaporate one of those tubes and set fire to the whole back of the set.

Science explains everything, strings of teachers would later tell me. The world is no secret, and everything can be understood in this glorious century with the turn of a page in any good book. Don't lie awake at night and wonder, don't try to make connections between things; connections rise from ignorance and sure enough, ignorance spawns fear. No, everything operates in and of itself, and that was all there was to it. But I was nine, and the world had yet to unleash these things. Science had yet to encroach upon my dreams, my nightmares; the world had yet to focus from its blur. So connections were made, and Schmidt had, in my mind, surely and single-handedly put an end to our television set, and, despite my father cursing the burned wires and the sour smoke, despite the worry from my mother at the top of the stairs and my having to retreat to my room and my AM radio, I came to understand the world was full of gods, and some played baseball.

Our father was taken to the hospital just after the Phillies were eliminated from the post-season in the fall of 1978. I don't remember much about the pains swelling up in him or about his crash over the TV tray, or the stretcher coming through the living room, its wheels in rattle, just as the rain let up. After the rescue men barged into the foyer, our mother sent us to our room, made us shut the the door, and had us turn up our radio to drown out any possible tragedy. She didn't want us to see the terror there on the carpet: my father sprawled out in a field of broken beer glass, his eyes glazed up like Vaseline, his hoagie half-eaten with its parts disseminated on the rug. She was shielding us from memory. I still, however, vividly recall, not hours before, the tenth inning of Game Four. Maddox had lost the ball in the lights; it had dropped and rolled behind him, and the Dodger Stadium crowd exploded into a frenzy as Lopes crossed the plate with the winning run. We sank into the cushions of defeat. My father just sat there, didn't say a word, and stared at the set from within his own universe, as if to burn a hole into the stadium the size of his disappointment. I remember thinking his silence kind of odd and why he hadn't, over the course of the post-game chatter, at least tossed the remainder of his beer at the champagne-drenched Lasorda or something. He was holding it all back; that frightened me more than anything.

Psychologists say that keeping things inside you does physical damage, and that's why you've got to let it all out. They've documented cases of ulcers, liver failures, heart attacks, gall bladder infections, spleen disorders, rectal abominations, bone decay, and a host of other maladies attributed directly to stewing on the inside way too long. My father had been through the playoff wars before with his Phillies but had reacted quite differently than in this post-season. Up until his accident, he still talked about the great collapse of '64, when, deep into September, his beloved team blew a six-and-a-half game lead with twelve to play by losing ten straight. Once in a while late at night, filled on beers and angry reminiscence, he would go to his shoe box in the top of the closet and pull out the World Series tickets that he had prematurely bought from the milkman. "Ruiz stealing home... that was the killer," he would slur on cue, waving the yellowed Phillies logos at us there on the couch and pointing to a fictitious October date in which they would have played their game. Just the previous October, we had all watched in horror as Luzinski misplayed a ball off the left field wall that allowed the Dodgers to make a remarkable ninth-inning comeback. My father screamed at Ozark during that one, his face red with anger, the veins of his neck rising from his skin in a glorious blue river. "You stupid idiot, why didn't you put Martin out there? Defensive replacement... ninth inning...common sense. Ozark, what the hell were you thinking? Jesus Christ I can't believe what I'm seeing." He tore through the Phillies through most of that off-season, calling for the head of Ozark, calling Luzinski a fat pig, and demanding trades into his sports page over the winter meetings.

My father died shortly after he lapsed into a coma in December 1978. I expected a solid explanation from my mother or even my older brother, who at twelve I expected would now have an added burst of wisdom. They needed to tell me something—anything—of some disease that had rotted away dad's insides from drinking too much beer, or of some rare throat cancer that had started growing around his larynx and couldn't be stopped. I didn't know much about medical things; all I knew was that people got sick for any number of reasons and died. But I also knew that doctors could usually explain things to other adults, and those adults could, in turn, translate those answers into language that nine-year-old boys could understand. But my mother's relentless sobs offered no translation; she only shook her head and opened her arms in question to the sky. So I made connections once again, and I came to hate Gary Maddox because his dropped ball had gone right through my father's insides and tore a giant hole that couldn't be plugged. I also understood why my father had sat there so silent: the Phillies had worked him up so much the year before, on that dreadful black October night of 1977, that he didn't have anything left to shout. He was almost inviting death by sipping calmly on his backwash, and Maddox must have seen right through the wires and the tubes and the glass and decided the job was his.

In the Spring of 1979, my mother pulled us out of school to visit our Aunt Bernice in Dunedin, Florida. She still hadn't gotten over our father's death, and Billy rode in the front seat to give her directions down I-95 and console her if a sobbing fit started up. The car still rattled, for my mother hadn't gotten around to getting the muffler hitched right. Just last summer, after eight beers, my father had crawled under the car with a coat hanger to "fix the rusty pipes." He had twisted the coat hanger into one long wire and, after a good hour, came out from beneath the car pronouncing that he had kept the muffler from touching the ground. However, he had haphazardly frapped the muffler to the frame, and now, every time the car dipped, the wires would swing down and a trail of sparks would roll along behind us. It was just another of my father's legacies; unfortunately, my mother was all too aware of this, and every time after the car dipped and she happened to glance in the rear-view mirror to see the sparks, Billy would have to go for the Kleenex's in the glove box. I suppose she was putting off fixing the muffler because it would take away one more memory; it would be the mechanic's muffler then, not my father's anymore.

Dunedin's lawns are mostly sand, and those who yearn for plush green grass usually waste a lot of time planting and watering and waiting for the seed to come in evenly. Aunt Bernice, after years of such fruitless yearning, ripped up her sod and hammered down Astro-Turf from one fence post to the other. It was rather startling, a plastic oasis of sorts, given that every other house on Barry Street sat back on lawns bare of anything remotely green. She had wedged a Virgin Mary statue in some stones just along the walk, though the thing was plastic and had trouble holding back the spring winds.

My mother cried at Aunt Bernice's kitchen table for most of the vacation, leaving Randy and me with little to do except stare at the glass eggs in the living room and have an occasional catch with our cousin's old soccer balls out of the walk-in closet. Our excessive boredom didn't really concern my mother too much, who was too absorbed by her bitterness at being left a widow, without a life insurance check, who would need to raise two sons on the income of a cashier. Aunt Bernice, however, after several bouts of consolation, finally surveyed us there under her glass eggs and suggested a drive over to Clearwater, where we could see the Phillies in spring training.

Randy's enthusiasm exceeded mine, and for good reason. He had just signed up for another year of baseball at Milbourne, and this year he was expected to pitch. They all said he had a hell of an arm out of left—an arm that could peg a runner at the plate— and the pitching instructor was promising him some development from the mound. Besides that, however, and more importantly, Randy had not made The Connection and so firmly etched it into his brain as I had done. For me, watching baseball again, especially the Phillies, would mean a return to that living room rug with my father prone across the broken glass. Florida or not, new season or not, it was still the Schmidt home run and the imploded set, still the dropped ball and the hole in my father's insides, which came back at me like newborn fire.

"Two thirds of the earth is covered by water," Randy started. "The rest...."

"Is covered by Gary Maddox," I said on cue. I didn't want to think about any of that, especially of the man who had killed my father, but Randy had just put it out there, as if he knew what I wanted to avoid but that I was nevertheless programmed to respond.

"Hell of a range," he said. "Some days when his feet are extra quick you can probably put him out there alone." Randy appreciated any good fielder, but he was already thinking in the past about all of that. He considered himself an ex-outfielder now, and as he sat silent for the remainder of the ride, I knew he was tinkering in his head with the change-up he would need to work on when we got back home.

Psychologists say that acting on impulse is a healthy and natural thing. The brain acts accordingly when given a situation in which a snap decision must be made, when the factors, deep beneath the surface, weigh themselves in milliseconds, send a message to the brain, and then generate response through physical action. I suppose all of that pertained to me that morning when Maddox came out of the tunnel, and, before Randy could get his pen and hat over the rail, I tugged at the center fielder's sleeve and screamed, "You killed my father. I hate you. Why did you kill my father?" Everyone who had heard my outburst, including several dozen fans, my brother, my aunt, several Phillies, Maddox, and especially me, was quite surprised to hear such a thing out of a nine-year-old boy's mouth. Maddox stepped back, as if to play a ball that had fallen in front of him, his eyes wide in disbelief. Randy's pen dropped to the dirt, and the shouts that surrounded my sudden burst had now eased like a low tide into silence. I felt alone, suspended by a thread above the earth, as if, just like my father in his moment of that Phillies loss, I inhabited my own universe.

"You...killed him," I said, almost beneath my breath, but loud enough to re-emphasize. And a sea of fans swept me then, along with Randy and my aunt., into obscurity as Maddox, along with Bowa, McBride, Boone, Lerch, and the red running blurs of other names made their way across the grass. I was suddenly nothing, a kid fading ten rows back into a crowd, a kid who had expelled his insides, dumped them right there in Clearwater, two thousand miles away from his own living room. Aunt Bernice, who seemed to understand— though I could not understand how she could— pulled me by the elbow to the metal bleachers, patted me on the head, and sat me down. Randy, seated on her opposite side, didn't even look at me; nervously his eyes shifted to the dirt along the foul line, where he would spend a good three innings searching for his lost pen.

The summer of 1979 was long and hot and silent. The Butterworth's house caught fire on a Sunday at the end of July because Mrs. Butterworth had left some bacon grease going on the stove. It caught the frilly curtains and that's all that was needed to burn up everything else—the kitchen, the living room with the big color television set, even half of the new addition which Mr. Butterworth had cursed into existence. We watched from the swing set at the playground, fascinated by the fire, by the firemen, by the reporters shoving microphones into the calamity. It was a scene filled with loss and desperation, and, after the last flames had been doused and the night and the crickets returned, the whole thing just made me feel hollow and empty with nothing and no one to turn to. Our mother, though her bouts of weeping had let up, was prone to long periods of silence now. She would stay in her room for the most part, where she had plugged in the old black- and- white console and had begun, from seven a.m. or so on, to indulge in marathons of daytime soaps and such.

Day by day in a succession of sweltering weeks, Randy battered the side of the tool shed with his change-ups. I caught for him several times in the early part of the summer, but I didn't have a catcher's mitt and wound up tearing my old glove up after some of his fastball sessions. Then he got me in the groin with a low- and-away pitch, and while I writhed in pain on the burned grass, he just stood sixty feet away and marveled at his ability to make that particular pitch drop out of the strike zone. That's when I quit as catcher. Through most of July and all of August, between his pleads for me to come back out, I spent the afternoons lying across my bed just listening——clank, clank, clank, clank—as his pitches dented the tin two stories below.

The Phillies were awful that summer. Everyone expected them to make it to the Series because they had gotten Rose, the final piece of the puzzle. I knew better, however. Maybe it was something in the eyes of Maddox, of those other players, something I had put into motion that spring morning down in Clearwater. I felt it first on the drive home, an assurance that I had deposited a sort of karma that would descend on Maddox and his team for taking my father's life. They were going to suck was all I kept thinking to myself, Rose or no Rose. Even Randy had given up listening or watching on the evenings the games were televised. He was busy struggling as a pitcher himself, obsessed with getting his throws over the plate. His coach had put him back in the outfield for the last part of the season because he had given up a ton of runs and all of his pitches had lost their velocity. His arm had become weak; even as an outfielder, his throws to the plate now skipped across the infield grass. So, in the last days of summer, after the baseball season had faded to painful memory and then into the school year, Randy turned to FM radio. He had begun to grow his hair long past his shoulders and to buy albums full of electric guitar solos, anticipating no doubt the void of adolescence that loomed like a monster in front of him.

Handling grief is a tricky thing, no less tricky than some of those splendid circus stunts that trapeze artists perform hundreds of feet above the ring. It requires balance, repose, a sense that the other side can be reached, that solid ground is but a wire-walk away. But you must not look down; you must never consider that a sea of gawking spectators is waiting for that fatal step and for your inevitable plunge downward. I feared that my mother, and now my brother, had, in fact, looked down. She never said more than a sentence or two at the dinner table now, and, after some meek orders to load the dish machine, she would retreat back into her shell of television in the top room, gently closing her door, forcefully shutting off the outside world. Randy had begun to hang out at the construction site of the new mall with unfamiliar boys in leather; he reeked of cigarette smoke and couldn't bring himself to look up from his plate before he was out the door. He was headed for trouble no doubt: a runaway to some Canadian province, some time on mind drugs, asleep beneath a bridge every night beside a burned-out fire.

In the summer of 1980, when the crickets were in full force, I could hear above their drone the faint sobs out of my mother's room. I was eleven now, though I felt much older, as if the world for the past two years, like some archaic merry-go-round, had slowed to a dead crawl. They say those kinds of things happen in car accidents, where several seconds stretch themselves out into an eternity of minutes. Since my father's death, the two years had tumbled by like a century. So here I was, eleven going on a hundred and twelve, and in my ancient wisdom I felt compelled to go down the hall to open my mother's door. She was there on the bed, in nothing but the blue light of the set and bathed in the glistening aftermath of a good cry. Then I was at the edge of her bed, getting her to turn her head from the eleven o'clock news and asking her what could possibly be wrong.

"Oh. it's everything Billy," she sobbed. "I'm so tired of being a cashier, of keeping up with the bills, of trying to keep this house. I'm just…tired." She turned away to allow a wave of sobs to descend, feeling the vast expanse of the bed which she alone had inhabited for two years.

"Mom," I said. "You know Randy will be old enough to get a job soon. I was hearing him talk about some guy who wanted to hire him to guard the lumber up at the new mall they're building."

She turned and smiled through her veil of water. "Three dollars an hour won't do much, Billy."

"But that's only the start, mom. He'll get better jobs, and then me, too. We'll help, we'll work together and help."

Two years of silence and pain and wisdom drew my hand across the bed to console her, and then I told her I loved her, possibly for the first time ever. She smiled at that, too, and I felt somehow that I had gotten through, that some long-constructed barrier had been invisibly brought down. She wasn't looking down anymore: she could see the platform up ahead, the place where the tightrope ended. She could see us all getting out of this mess: she would take that manager position at the coffee shop that she was so afraid to touch; she would meet a man and bring him home to us; he would take us for ice cream sundaes and rides on the Tilt-A-Whirl at St. John Boscoe's carnival and on day trips to the Jersey shore, where we might accidentally, and then permanently, call him "dad." Randy would get his hair cut short and the guitar albums would collect dust; he would get a job in the new mall and try out for the American Legion team, maybe even pitch with an arsenal of change-ups and sliders and win a few games on pure grit.

In the space of silence between us, the sports anchor had come on to explain a 6-5 Phillies loss. They had dipped into third place on a crucial eighth inning error by Maddox; his relay throw had sailed well over Schmidt's head, allowing Carter to score as the Expos moved into first The reporters had Maddox pinned against his locker, a towel draped around his neck to catch the flowing perspiration. "I can't explain it," he sighed. "We're better than this, I know we're better than this." In those seconds following, the reporter said nothing. Instead, he let the dead air fester like an untreated wound. I looked into the television then as Maddox looked back, his eyes full of disgust and resignation.

"It will be alright," I said, speaking to my mother, but speaking also to him through the tubes and the wires and the glass. I forgave Maddox at that moment for killing my father."Things will come around."

If the Phillies had not won the World Series in 1980...if Schmidt had not hit that dramatic moon shot in the tenth inning of a game in Montreal on the last weekend of the season to clinch the division...if four out of the five games of the National League Championship Series with the Astros had not gone extra innings...if Maddox himself had not driven in the go-ahead run to win Game Five and send the Phillies to the Series or if he had not caught the last out and rode his teammates shoulders to the infield...if Schmidt had not gotten MVP of the World Series and brought the Phillies their first world championship in ninety-seven years...if all of that had not happened in the months that followed that moment of consolation in my mother's room, I might have taken Science more seriously at school. I might not have failed and repeated, failed and repeated, all the way through grade school, through high school, through Biology and Chemistry and one frustrated teacher after another. When the multiple choice tests came around, I might have thought long and hard and drew some facts out of textbook pages I had memorized beneath lamps and had come to know so well, so certain would I have been of the world and its consequences, things that could be analyzed, weighed, and explained by the touch of a pen.

Instead I circled "none of the above," or "all of the above," on every Science test I took. When Mr. Petri, late in my senior year, confronted me in the lab about it, I had to explain that I couldn't understand how anyone could be so sure of anything, that "the above" I circled came to mean that all things were connected in ways which we could never know. The petals of a flower and a dying star, igneous rock and the song of a beached whale, ocean tides and the tears of a mother, a waning gibbous moon and the murdering orgy of a madman, a long home run deep to right and an imploded television set in a living room twenty miles away, a dropped ball and a father's life, a championship after a ninety-seven year drought and a new father riding in the waves, were all hopelessly and inexplicably intertwined. I told a befuddled Mr. Petri that science stops making sense after a point, and the world operates outside the laws of physics and instead becomes governed entirely by the laws of baseball. The "above," I told him, was saying all of these things, and it also meant that I didn't know anything at all—but then, neither did he, Science teacher or not. "At least I'm one step ahead of you because I'm on to it" I said. "I've seen the connections you know. Seen them, been through them."

Mr. Petri shook his head and sighed his sigh, turned off the gas, put the tubes away in their sheaths, called me a little smart-ass, and sent me with a pink slip to the principal.

CHRIST FIGURES

ALL OF THE PEOPLE burning in hell are absolutely surprised that they are sent there. Millions upon millions, piled like stones, fight away the shock, because in each of their minds they must have reasoned that whatever acts they committed while alive were completely justified, but now here they are in eternal flame. To get to hell, all you have to do is be evil, and that includes manipulative women, greedy salespeople, and just about any car mechanic uptown.

Johnny Sanford is going to be one of those surprised people. He's going to hell riding a wave as fast and furious as his Camaro and filled with a total misconception of the universe. He hasn't murdered anyone or conspired to destroy office buildings or hired a gunman to take out his girl friend because she thought about another man. But he's buried in sneakiness and filled with depravity. Everything he does he does to ruin, yet in every sense—just like Hitler must have thought as he was holed up in his bunker as the Allies closed in—he absolutely believes himself to be a saint. Saint Johnny of Belfield he'll be anointing himself as he rides his wave downward.

Back in '78, I joined the Mustang League with Johnny, who had spent a lot of hours pounding baseballs off the tool shed in his back yard, which made him much more ready than me. After two weeks of tryouts in the rain, the coach penciled him in as lead-off hitter, and in the first game of the season he hit a triple but was thrown out at the plate after he blew a stop sign by the third base coach. I couldn't get over that. Here he was, in his very first game and very first at-bat outside of pitches in the dirt and occasional games with the neighborhood kids, and he deliberately ignored the advice of his assistant coach and got himself pegged at the plate. Then, filled with audacity, he jawed with the teen-aged ump, who no doubt was equally as shocked as Coach Delpino standing at first base. Johnny wouldn't take "out" for an answer, even after coach pulled him off the diamond by his sleeve and sat him behind the chain-linked fence for three innings.

Maybe Johnny would have shut up had his mother or father come to see him. I could sense his envy of the other boys, who all went up swinging to whispers of advice from fathers standing behind the backstop or who were urged on to first base by the screams of ranting mothers pumping their arms from the metal bleachers or consoled by both if they went down swinging. Johnny had no one, save a dying grandfather over in Chelsea with burned-out eye sockets. I suppose not having anyone who cared is what, in his own mind, gave him license to turn up the gas as he headed around third. No one was going to scold him on a car ride home, nor send him to his room without an ice cream dessert, nor lecture him on the proper way to behave when a teen-aged umpire called him out of there.

Sometimes in bed at night, and sometimes on long bus rides where the traffic backs up on Midvale and the afternoon sun throws squares of light across the seats and gets the businessmen miserable and sighing long and loud, I think about the birth of evil. Even on hot afternoons where the sweat beads like little crystal jewels on the foreheads of those irritable strangers, that kind of thought makes me shiver. I shiver in the middle of August afternoons on crowded buses because I always get to thinking about Johnny Sanford sitting behind that chain-linked fence for three long error-filled innings—well over an hour of baseball— before Mr. Delpino let him back in. For Johnny, that's where his evil was born. Thoughts, tilled from anger and loneliness, from the emptiness of a fatherless backstop and motherless bleachers, fertilized his brain into a raging thicket of man-eating ivy. I remember his eyes: little coals that burned holes in the outfield grass. He sat motionless and transfixed like the models in my art classes I would later work to sketch.

Never moving a muscle, not even to breathe: his mind had drifted off, perhaps thinking about the way things should be— the home run he should have notched, the mother and father who should be congratulating him, the friends who should have rustled his hair and called him the hero of the first inning. Now, the innings Johnny missed deposited only seeds of bitterness into his little skull. All of the boys (I don't remember even one of their names) were too afraid to even go down that far on the bench. Even Delpino and the third base coach whispered amongst themselves about how they should handle angry burning eyes like that and came to the same conclusion as the boys: stay away from them. Perhaps that too allowed Johnny's personal evil to sprout—unfettered, untouched, fertilized in the vacuum of his mind with no moral compass to douse the flame. Maybe all Johnny needed was a hand on his shoulder and a 'nice triple' from someone who even pretended to care.

That was near twenty years ago. I don't remember the score or who won the thing, in fact nothing at all past those first three innings of Johnny's torment. The faces have all been lost, faces never to be recalled, boys who signed up and played a season or two seasons or three seasons and then disappeared back into the crowded hallways of elementary schools and long carnival lines. Only Johnny's eyes stay with me, burned harder and more permanent than any summer grass and lingering like the light from flash bulbs long after I've closed my eyes. I see that bottled anger in him still, twenty years subdued and barely perceptible, but still there. Now, when I am awake and working, I see it when he calls his quarter-till meetings and goes on and on about proper service and food cost and how a restaurant employee should behave when the wait gets to two hours. He played ball with no soul, and now he manages with no soul, working without conscience for some noble corporate cause that might someday get him somewhere and in the process rid the world of imperfection.

The thing that perpetuates evil—that is, those with no souls—is that no one recognizes it. Unfettered and subdued, it grows like hidden bone cancer, and those too quick to point it out are never taken seriously, even castigated and sent to their mythical rooms without supper. At The Char House, only I notice Johnny as the devil, and so I am trapped on my own little island to figure out how to convince the world of my vision.

"He's o.k.," Timmy said when I brought up his evil ways, and then he just flipped his grill and eyed the spices falling from the shelf, perhaps deep in thought, perhaps oblivious to any sort of thought considered deep. I never knew what he was thinking in those nine-plus years. He never reacted; he just kept pressing the steaks until every bit of juice was gone and there was no doubt that they were well done. Management, especially Johnny, didn't like re-cooks, so Timmy was their man.

They bring the lobster shipments in on Thursdays around three; on one particular Thursday there was some sort of traffic accident out on the parkway involving the delivery truck and several subcompacts. That was all the information we received, and so of course I felt compelled to embellish the whole thing and explain to the wait staff that the truck had toppled and spilled hundreds of lobsters across six lanes of highway, prompting motorists to stop and lay claim to the crawling meals—which, I reminded the waiters, were thirty-two dollars apiece on the menu. I explained that the injuries incurred from the accident were largely the result of lobster bites, including some severed fingers and a bleeding ass. I suppose I have some acting blood in me; my father had once suggested I take up some classes or get myself to Manhattan for some auditions. People believe near everything I tell them until they discover I'm just trying to have a good time. The way I see it, a lie is only o.k. if it is told to entertain.

"I'll need to see you in the storage room when you get a chance," Johnny said after word of my embellishments had drifted from the waiter hole. He didn't like the idea that I had put one over on his wait staff and he mentioned it to me as I was stocking up on take-out containers. He wanted me to feel awful because they had bought my fable, and there was no place for fibs in his establishment. He didn't care to hear that it was all in good fun.

"There's no room for funny stuff in this business. You need to take cooking as seriously as you can," he said beneath the crackers. "A serious kitchen is a happy kitchen."

I was always derided by the waitresses, particularly Patti—and the busboys, too—for mass-murdering the crustaceans. I told them that I had read somewhere that lobsters had the highest I.Q.'s in the sea next to dolphins. "In an article in Scientific American—October '84, if memory serves, they hooked up some wires and a calculator to their antennas and had found them to be able to do simple addition," I explained, reeling them in. "Yep, they found one exceptionally large twenty-five-pound specimen off the coast of Newfoundland, near seventy years old and pre-dating the Eisenhower Administration, who could even manage light calculus." They were justly horrified as I boiled their brains in the front pot. "It's my job, and I don't question orders...just like Calley slaughtering villagers in My Lai or something. Can't break the chain of command or the restaurant will go under. Poor Johnny would lose his job. And besides poor Johnny, I hate math."

I brought Shelley to tears one evening when I suggested we test whether a lobster could write. I placed a pencil into its crusher claw, then lined a blank sheet of paper beneath it. She scoffed as I stood there with my hand on my chin waiting for the lobster to begin, and then as she looked away to a party being seated in her station, I quickly scrawled 'help me' and moved away from the crustacean. She turned, read the message, and screamed, then broke into tears as I criticized the lobster's sloppy cursive because it wasn't "Catholically correct." I dropped the thing into the boiling water and watched it change orange.

Late one night just after last call, after Neal had gone home to throw up his guts, Patti approached my barstool in the corner of O'Shinns. She had had her share of whatever, and the rage in her drunken demeanor had obviously been stored all night just for me. "Karma," she slurred. I had never heard 'karma' slurred before, so she secured my attention.

"Beg your pardon?"

"There's such a thing, karma." She had to balance herself against the bowling machine and re-focus. The lights came up and she got uglier.

"You're not going to start in on the lobster thing," I said. I had a few Molsons in me, and I wasn't in the mood to re-visit.

"You're going to come back as a.... crustacean." I was surprised she articulated the word.

"Yeah I know... and some cook in some restaurant is going to boil me and that will be that."

"How about worse...how about you're going to fall out of a truck on the parkway and be run over by a fucking tractor trailer...karma's not going to get you for killing all those...." She leaned and thought under the glare.

"Lobsters," I finished.

"Karma's going to get you for lying to me."

I took Patti home and had some terrific sex with her that night. She complained I smelled like fish, and I didn't want to make the obvious comeback, so I let her fall to sleep with most of the sheets and the extra pillow. Generally, I needed two pillows to sleep soundly, but I figured I needed to make up for the lie, which, come to think of it, I never should have felt guilty about in the first place, because, like I said, I was just out to entertain. I did, however, have some lobster salad in a dream, which I still can't seem to interpret except to say that I've never tried lobster salad (mayonnaise has given me stomach pains since I was four). Some might say a lobster dream, even of the salad variety, might be out of guilt and that it was a little subconscious warning for me to stop boiling the things. Some might say it was just what was on my mind as I drifted off and that if I had eaten anything decent after the bar and the beers, well I might have had another dream entirely. I like to believe that it meant nothing at all. Dreams have no meaning in the real world of orders coming in and steaks to be loaded on the grill and live lobsters to be dropped into pots and lectures to be listened to in the backs of storage rooms. I like to believe it was because I was missing the extra pillow.

I had a history of fibbing, but the lies were unlike the general web of deceit that Johnny was spinning around the entire establishment. I was only meaning to bring laughter and try to make the long hours shorter back there behind the line. Behind the line. It got so hot sometimes in the summers, especially when the air conditioning wasn't cooling the dining room. We would need to soak rags in ice water and drape them around our necks. Johnny made sure we kept our sleeves to our heavy chef coats rolled down so that we'd look professional to the guests lining up at the salad bar. With exhibition broiling, you had to put on an act. The only way to condense the long hours and forget about the heat was by jokes. James, our end man who was responsible for making the potatoes and running stock and adding the extra insult as waiters walked away with their trays, had to have a seat in the back one evening because the one hundred twenty degree heat had gotten to him. Johnny was kind enough to send Billy Billows, his dining room manager, into the break room with a tall Coke and some pineapple chunks before ordering the overheated James back into the inferno.

Poor Billy Billows. He had just been transferred from Fort Myers, but he was just another luckless bastard with whom Johnny had had his way, just another in a long chain of yes-men under Johnny's command. Billy didn't know it, but he was in for a long ride working ninety- hour weeks on a salary that would wind up to about three dollars an hour.

Johnny can make anybody do anything, I was convinced. He had power to conform dishwashers, hostesses, waiters, salad bar people, managers, seafood vendors, customers, cooks. In some ways, he still has that power over me. How else to explain? Here it is twenty years after the ball games, and here I stay on at The Char House with Johnny as my manager. Sometimes I think I am hypnotized, that Johnny is dangling some unknown precious object in front of me that throws me into some kind of trance. I get ready, I drive down the parkway, I clock in, I work in stifling heat for ten hours, I clock out. Though I've thought about quitting every single day for nine years and five months while I pound my Molsons at O'Shinns, while I go off to sleep, and while I watch a lot of bad television in the afternoons before the sun in the window tells me it's time to go, the simple fact is that, year after year, I get ready, I drive down the parkway, I clock in, I work in stifling heat for ten hours, I clock out.

The summer heat is the worst. Johnny told all of us at his quarter-till meeting one day that the Char House building was simply too big to cool off. He had placed twenty fans between the tables to cool off the guests, and he told us that there was nothing much to be done when the temperature reached a hundred outside. "Air conditioning is meant for small rooms and such," he said. I raised my hand in the back, which he was slow to acknowledge, whereupon I mentioned that the temperature in Houston was over a hundred nearly every day and how do you explain the air-conditioned Astrodome? Huh? After the chuckles died down and the doors opened for business, he took me into the inner office during the whole first rush and Timmy had to take my place on the line. Johnny suspended me for two weeks without pay for my "positively little remark." He wanted to fire me right there under the binders, but then I convinced him that good cooks were rare commodities and that he and I both knew I was good, and that I'd put too much time in and that I would be sorely missed by the senior staff. Besides that, I said, we go all the way back to little league. That bit of pleading saved me my job.

One of the managers from several years back, Robbie Cidori, joined me for some Molsons at O'Shinns during my suspension. I saw him browsing the tobacco shops along South Street looking for some quality cigars, so I invited him my way. I came to look at my suspension as a good thing, because now I had the opportunity to catch up on some much-needed drinking, some possible tinkering with my Chevette, and a major cleaning-out of my refrigerator. It didn't take much prodding to get Robbie to a bar stool. He was married and living over in Behemoth with a third child on the way. He had left The Char House under mysterious circumstances two years before when, one day when we all looked up, he simply wasn't there anymore. Johnny, nor the other managers, ever offered any explanation for his disappearance. In fact, they acted as if he was never even there. Every one of them changed the subject when Robbie's name was brought up. You could see it mostly in Billy Billows' eyes: something was secret, and if word got out, firings would begin. Waiters whispered in their stations about Robbie's' vanishing act, and there were extra meetings in the inner office which no doubt dealt with his demise. Robbie Cidori was a heavy man, weighing in at a good three hundred, so I did my part in the whole mystery by writing "Missing" on a gallon of milk, along with a drawing of his face. I slid my artwork into the cooler in one of the waiter holes, where it quickly was chuckled at, and then it too disappeared, just like Robbie.

"Had Zach on the way," Robbie said. Barry had poured him a shot of Denaka. "Just near Christmas two years back. The wife called me during one of our Christmas party slams, told me the contractions were twenty minutes apart and I'd better come get her." Robbie downed a shot and took off his glasses. "Johnny, fucking Johnny. I tell him about it and you know what he says? 'We need you here,' he says. 'I've got a thirty top and a forty top being seated and I need you... we can't do this thing without you' Yeah well my wife needs me more I says and then he screams that I'd better decide what's more important, my job or my family. My family of course I says, and then he looks right at me like I just took a rifle and shot his dog. Then he comes real close, and now I'm thinking this guy is going to wail me or something and I clench my fists ready to defend myself. He gets really close and he whispers in an eerie calm 'I want you the hell out of my establishment.'"

"So that's where you went. Off to be a family man."

"Right down the steps, pushing my way through the thirty top, the forty top, knocking some guests over like bowling pins, right out into zero degrees without my jacket." He slammed another shot of Denaka and shifted his big ass back to the center of the stool. "But not to worry. The wife got me a leather jacket for Christmas. And Zach...and then Marie, and now...."

"And now you're working on your third kid."

"And my third shot." Robbie motioned for Barry at the end of the bar.

It's always good to hear when somebody gets out. It's almost like a prison break, and the longer you stay, the more difficult it becomes to plan escape routes. Robbie had made it over the wall. He was living in a big rancher over in Behemoth and selling restaurant equipment for Saxon. He had settled into a nice normal life, and only occasionally, with a third child on the way for instance, did he feel a need to go out and get some cigars and then drink himself blind. I apologized to Robbie because I had never gotten to know him while he managed and that he seemed like an o.k. guy and that things had worked out best for him this way, despite the toppled guests. I apologized because I was still there and promised him that I would find a way out. I asked him if there was a position over at Saxon, but he just stared into the bottles.

"But you shouldn't have to find a way out," he said. "The Char House should be a good place, a fun place. You should want to work there forever."

"But Johnny Sanford."

"But Johnny Sanford." Robbie lowered his voice, as if the couple seated at the end of the bar were going to try to listen. "They've got restaurant unions you know, ways to get rid of guys like him. That's what unions are for, to protect poor employees like you. Restaurant socialism if you will."

"I'd never get anybody on my side," I said. "Everyone's either too afraid or they say they don't mind the guy. He hides his evil too well. There's no way to battle hidden evil."

"I suppose you're right. Maybe you need to get over that wall. Don't come down to Saxon, though. I don't want to be held responsible for your getting out. Johnny wouldn't take too kindly. I know you're a damn good cook, and I wouldn't want to steal that away from Johnny."

"Why would you care?" I was surprised to see a fear overcome him suddenly. He shifted and squirmed and made the wooden stool creak. He sighed.

"Johnny has control of more than just that restaurant," he said. "They order from Saxon for one. I can guarantee you that account would be canceled if he found out you and I were working there, and they'd trace that back to me. The thing is, nobody knows I'm down there right now and I want to keep it that way. I've got a third one on the way and I need to keep it that way."

Robbie finished up suddenly, as if a wall of fear were mounting so quickly that it could only be scaled by getting up right then and there from his stool and leaving the bar. He said his good-byes, and when he walked out the door, I was quite sure that I would never see him again. He was going back into the euphoria of family life, shedding the last layer of skin that was Char House.

As I left the bar after two that Sunday morning, I kept thinking how terrific the world would be with unions everywhere. I was thinking about how I could possibly sway the masses and get them to vote union. And the more I thought "union," the more I thought "no way." I would need a majority vote and I could not think of even one employee who would risk everything as I was about to do. They find a way to fire you and make sure you have a black mark on you forever if you try to bring a union in. They make sure you learn your lesson.

I was tired as I started up my tired old car, and I was looking forward to getting home and going to sleep and dreaming about a world without Johnny, a world where I could joke and pull pranks, a world where waiters could be free to laugh without worrying about who was watching them, a world where husbands could go off to watch their wives have babies, a world where I wouldn't need to disgrace the sides of milk cartons anymore because nobody would ever be missing and everybody would want to stay.

On Sunday mornings with a heavy hangover, it is especially difficult to discipline church into my schedule. I managed to get to St. Anselm's twice a month or so, and even then, all during Mass, all I could think about was getting home to get some rest before I had to go in for the Sunday slam. But I felt the need for church on Sundays, or perhaps it was programmed into my existence from the time I first learned to fold my hands in my Communion suit.

Father Holmes, near ninety now, started his sermon every Sunday with the peace sign raised over the congregation. With his sagging cheeks and thinning hair line, he looked a little like Nixon as he departed the presidency and walked across the South Lawn towards the helicopter. Father Holmes spoke in whispers, as if the Word of God were some secret that could not pass beyond the hallowed statues of St. Anselm and the Virgin Mary onto 676. He seemed to be looking right at me today, as if he knew that my head was hurting and that all I wanted to do was lay down and quit. Listen because it's not quite so obvious he said. The Word comes in all forms, not just in lines out of a Bible. Open your ears to things God wants from you, to things you need to do for Him to carry on. Listen to Him as you're taking your showers, as you're blow drying your hair or rolling down your car windows to let in the summer air. Listen to him as the crickets die and the rain comes up, and as you try to bring on sleep, restless as you might be. Don't shut Him out. He is there, talking to you between the lines of your life, between the seconds you build to make your days. God is telling you what to do if you only listen, for we are all Christ figures being crucified for the sins of others. He wants you to rid yourself of the evils of your life and to make the world a better place for your friends, your family, your children, yourself. Father Holmes whispered lower still: it is up to you to move the stone and rise. It is up to you to move the stone and rise.

I killed Johnny Sanford as he was crossing the parking lot to his brand-new Camaro. I was just sitting there warming up my '85 Chevette, hoping that the engine would get me home one more time and that I wouldn't need to put it in the garage with all the dishonest mechanics and take the bus again. I shifted into drive just as Johnny passed into my sightline, and I then I just pushed it for all it was worth. Just like that, like it wasn't me doing the accelerating at all, or it was me, nine years of me, all balled into one shining moment. I hit Johnny without any headlights. I was a three- thousand-pound apparition coming out of the night, and I sent him in a heap over the guardrail, broken and dead for sure. I didn't speed out of the lot, for I was certain no one had seen me. But I also didn't speed out because I felt this relief suddenly, like a touch of Anbesol on a raging toothache or a deep massage that relaxed my body all over, one so deep that it made me want to sleep and forget what things could really be like without pain. I drove the way I always did, with one foot over the brake pedal in case the car began to stall. I turned the headlights on and could see that the hood had been pushed up. It would be something I could fix with a good rubber mallet, though more than likely I would be ditching the car uptown and taking the J bus for a while. The car was in its last days anyway, and no one would be surprised when I told them the thing finally died.

As I drove the dark side streets—Catherine, Delancey, Christian, Piedmont, round and round— I thought about turning myself in and how difficult it would be to be funny anymore. I'd seen my father lose his sense of humor after my mother had died, and I imagined the same thing would settle into me—though Johnny could certainly not be compared to my mother, and my father didn't murder her like I had just done to this man. There would be an investigation with a sheet full of suspects, including me.

If they figured out Johnny's flesh trauma came from a Chevette bumper, it would mean time in prison, time away from my station behind the line. I sure would miss Timmy and James. I sure would miss those Saturday night slams that I'd managed to handle so well. I thought about that long and hard as I walked up South Street, then as I seated myself on the bar stool at O'Shinns, then through Molson after Molson as the clock moved toward two. Robbie Cidori had planted that idyllic vision of life after Johnny into my head, and I was looking forward to that life.

Life after Johnny. I thought more about that life than about his dead body dumped over the rail. With a couple more beers, my act came to mean nothing at all, or rather, it became just an act of consequence upon which the Char House tide would turn.

No, I wouldn't turn myself in. Prison was for criminals, for those who were getting what they deserved. And I didn't deserve prison, I deserved a decent life because I was and still am a decent person, a good person. Hell, all of us behind that dreadfully hot line were good people who deserved a decent life. Now I had cleansed the little world of Char House of one big piece of evil, and that little world, soon to be a brilliant green, would be more thankful. Timmy would thank me. James would thank me. The busboys and the waiters, one by one, would filter out of their stations to thank me. Billy Billows in his starched white shirt and his one rung up on the corporate ladder would thank me. Of course, I would never tell them that I had done it, but secretly they would know. They would know as surely as they knew that I was a prankster, and that lobsters really have no definable intelligence, and that all their broiler cook was boiling over the years were creatures without cerebral cortexes, creatures with no souls that couldn't feel any pain.

No pain. I relaxed and ordered another Molson, and though I knew the stomach-ache would surely come, I ordered, from the bar menu written in chalk, a lobster salad sandwich and a side of fries.

SURRENDER

AT NIGHT THEY smash their beer bottles on the pavement and ground their broken glass with their steel-toed boots until it becomes dust. I can hear them cursing in their drunken rages, whispering in the alley about promises of redemption. They are angry tonight, angrier than they have been in months. Perhaps it is the constant drizzle that has coated their jackets and turned the oil spots to slime beneath their feet. Perhaps they are waiting too long for trouble to arrive. No sirens have sounded, no lights have flicked on in the rooms above them, no voices have called out into the rain for them to cease their abrasions. In the silent interludes between their slurred profanities, I can sense them staring though my ground floor windows and fashioning a plan.

Mary died last week in the manner that I expected, though she lasted almost through the night. The doctors fed her enough medicine over the years, gallons I calculated, and one day we decided it would stop. Medicine didn't matter anymore, I told them— I was speaking for Mary, I was speaking for me. No use going on like this, trapped in a fog. Her eyes—they filled with life just before she went gray. Her last breath rose to the surface and illuminated her face like a moon just out of a cloud bank. Though she didn't speak, or even offer her hand to me as she passed, I knew she meant to apologize for putting me through so many nights. And she was thanking me, too, for not putting her through any more nights. She was saying all of that in her last flare of life; I could always read Mary's sighs like that.

The crickets crawl up under the floorboards and rub their legs together so that I can't sleep. I try to count them sometimes, separate their rubbings by distinctive chirps in the hope that I will tire and drift off. With so many thousands, I always lose count, and then the memories come rushing in to keep me awake, where the empty room above the floorboards makes me open my eyes. I can't see much except for the cracks of dimmed light beyond the drawn curtains, where the remaining streetlight knifes through the trickles. They'll probably get to that light, too, maybe tonight in the drizzle. All it will take is a heavy stone to put that last one out, leaving me in permanent darkness.

They would want that; that would dignify collective identity in such a dark place, milling about unseen behind the dumpsters, mingling the shuffle of their boots and the powdered glass sprinkled on the pavement with the ten thousand humming crickets. I should welcome these cave creatures, open my curtains and let them see into my room. There's nothing left to take, nothing to hide, so come see. Come see the unmade bed, the soiled sheets, the scattered papers, the frayed electrical wires, the broken sculpture of Dante, my shriveling form lying prone upon the bed. I would like them to bring their eyes to my window. Come. Come see me still consumed by Mary. She is there in the rain, she is there in the crickets, she is there in the planning whispers. Come see me still drowning by my dear departed Mary.

I need to get up and go to the window. I need to part the curtains.

The drizzle hypnotizes me into a deep trance and pins me to the mattress. The window just across the room is a thousand miles away, in another universe void of memory. I fight to escape, to get up, to cross my thousand- mile desert. But sleep arrives like soft falling water and I surrender. I close off the room and let the sound of the crickets ease me into a dream.

Mary lurks in the alley, a dark monolith rising from the heaps of shattered bottles not yet ground to dust. Her face betrays forty years of love, for it has sunk into the abyss of slurred profanity and drunken illusion that the alley holds like treasure. She forages in the dumpster. She calls me by name to help her find something lost beneath a mountain of refuse as she raises her dark arms. I cannot see her face, for the last streetlight has been shattered by a rock. I must go forth blind in my dream, where the cave creatures lurk in comfort and lay down their warnings like plush carpet. "Mary," I call louder, then louder still. The mountain descends, at first in a soft rain of crumpled paper, then in a wet avalanche of meat scraps, chicken bones, and broken glass. I am consumed, taken off my feet and down into suffocation. I cannot even call her name; she has been washed away in a sea of medicine, another gray body lost among the broken branches. "Mary," I call. "Mary."

They have pried open the front door with some of their tools. "Let's take him," I hear a voice, and then so many whispers like crickets congregating. They are rummaging through the things in my desk, looking for money, some of Mary's jewelry, a ticking watch, and vanished stones. But I have sold it all. Look and see: I have nothing left except the yellowed paper of memory. I wanted to show them, let them spy me here through the open curtains, so pathetic and empty and curled into a ball. Even now, as I hear them advance, I want to get up and slide open my window and call for help. Or escape. Or fight them off with my last shreds of strength. But I am still pinned to the bed by my dream, still lost looking for Mary. Even in the bare room I am searching the shadows for her revelation and waiting to be rescued.

Soon they will be down the hall to kick open my door. Five or six or seven of them will rush into the room, so full of liquor and covered in rain. They will close the door behind them. They will surround the bed and cover my mouth and say "hush." They will take me.

NED, STEVEN

NED AND STEVEN fished together every weekend for seventeen years. Ned hauled in the biggest pike and they made the newspaper.

NED BOUGHT A house in Fergusonville, stopped fishing, lost touch, led a separate and uninteresting life.

TWENTY YEARS AFTER they fished, they collided on a sidewalk.
    "Excuse me," Steven said.
    "Excuse me," Ned said.

JOEY'S HEAD

ONCE UPON AN August afternoon in the late sixties, I was hot and bored. My brain began to swell because I was thinking too hard about something to do. My brain was eleven. The summer sun had scorched all of the grass on the playground into an ugly brown straw, and I could see the waves of heat swirling up out of the dirt like some clear liquid was being siphoned from the earth, and it pissed me off. I don't know why I felt pissed off, and I still don't. Maybe I felt like it was the ideas of the day swirling away, and there was nothing I could do but watch. I sat along the shaded side of the sandbox, beneath the oak with the grown-over carved heart (Danny and Joanie are still married, I hear). I sat beside Joey Helmuth, my best friend. We kicked up the sand with our sneakers, dredging as if for oil, in our attempt to find an idea for the day. Joey didn't look pissed off at all, however.

I had worked my jaw into a slow, methodical ache from chewing a massive wad of bubble gum. It had been over an hour since the taste had gone out and the chemical properties of my saliva had now begun to transform the gum into a thick glue, made all the more gluey because I had eaten Saltines while I was chewing, and most of the crumbs had become trapped in the gum. This was the time I would normally spit the thing out (to see how far it might travel) or wedge it beneath the sandbox or wait until dinner to fasten it to the bottom of my chair. Instead, I nestled it firmly atop Joey's head. Suddenly vanquished from boredom and no longer pissed, I ran to the swings with my fists raised and my holler echoing to the woods. Fun!

Now I completely expected Joey to come running behind me with the wad fresh off his head and hurl it at me with full velocity— or pop it into his own mouth, even with the Saltine crumbs. I was not schooled in the viscosity of gum, especially with the added ingredients of a burning summer sun and uncombed blonde hair. I watched from behind motionless swings as Joey pulled long strings of gum into the air. I saw the pink stuff running down his outstretched arms. And the monstrosity grew upon his head like some mutated amoeba. Down it oozed between the follicles to the base of his skull, down the sides for his ears. Joey sat, quietly horrified, unaware of how bad things were going to be. "Get it off," was all he said, and in my recollection he must have said it a hundred or more times. "Get it off."

The more we worked, the worse it became, two sets of fingers picking away little pink slivers of glue, waiting for the wavy blond hair to return and for the world to be righted. There were little webs of gum littering the ground around us as we sat, a circle of gum and hair that must have looked like primitive primping. The afternoon sun sinking past the junk man's woods told us that removing all of the gum was a hopeless act. With no more sun, the cooler evening air cemented the remaining gum, like some hibernating organism, atop his skull.

"My mom's going to yell at you," Joey said, and then he started crying. He did not know what he looked like or indeed he would have cried a lot harder. Nevertheless, the tears rolled and the snot started running, and the combination of the red eyes, the wet face, the mucus, and the pink amoeba atop his head would have brought his mother crashing down in a heap of faint. So I wiped off his face with my sleeves and got him to brighten up a little when I lied and told him it didn't look "that bad."

It was getting late; the Butterworths had already been called to supper and the bugspray truck would be by soon. My heart beat fast: I was going to have to send Joey home with a pink head and I might be on the news. Then I had another idea: "I'll get some scissors from the house," I said. "We'll cut it away."

Joey grew apprehensive and backed away along the sandbox edge, breaking into a sniffle again, his eyes welling up the way they were. No one outside of a barber shop had touched his head with scissors before, I could tell, for his eyes concluded "you are no barber." He let me near his head when I finally convinced him that having a pink head might be fine for his sister Joanie, but it looked silly on a boy, and he would be laughed at all the way home, and no one would ever look at him the same again. So he stayed and I went inside my mother's sewing cabinet and I pulled out the scissors that had made my bedroom drapes, and I was careful to carry them so I wouldn't accidentally get stabbed to death.

Hooray! The scissors were sharp enough to cut through gum! I yanked Joey's skull down and sliced through the pink nightmare, chopping away sections of gum and hair with the inspired confidence of an expert barber, working away under the darkening trees until the glob became entirely dismembered from his head.

"It's all out, it's all out, we've done it," I exclaimed, stabbing the scissors into the sand.

It was only when Joey smiled across his dirty, tear-stained face that I realized a whole new monstrosity had been borne. Hair stuck out in every direction. The blonde bangs still hung down near his eyes, but they curved across his forehead like a brain wave. He was almost completely hairless on his left side. On the right side, long gobs of hair were slicked together and pointing straight out. In fact, there was only an inch or two of hair remaining on the back of his head that I had not radically altered. Outside of a brief respect for barbers, I was consumed by horror.

I thought about fixing his head up a little more, but it was getting dark for sure and I was being called to dinner, and it was spaghetti tonight. As much as I was looking forward to mom's sauce, it was not going to taste as good tonight because I knew that I was going to descend into in a crapload of trouble. Sure enough after dinner, the following sequence of events transpired: a) phone call from Mrs. Helmuth b) verbal spanking from Mom c) Dad arriving home late from work d) physical spanking from Dad e) Joey's older brother Eddie waiting outside to beat me up (and he was skilled in beating people up).

In recollection, I seem to have stayed inside the rest of that summer, coloring over things already colored, watching shows already watched.

The fear of Eddie was not so much about a physical beating than about the devious plan he would have lined up, a personalized plan just for me. As an example, when a kid in his class, just last term, took his favorite eraser from his desk on the way up for chocolate milk, Eddie stayed after class and loosened the legs of his desk and the next day, the kid came crashing down in a roar of laughter and books and had to have his jaw re-set. He later joked in the schoolyard, "You take my eraser, I eraser your face."

Eddie finally got to me one evening just before school started back, as I was hunting for crayfish down at the junkman's creek. I needed a break from living inside, and I just wanted another crayfish because my last one had died and I knew the rocks and where they were hiding, so I didn't need much time. As if anticipating my dead pet and knowing where I would come for the next one, Eddie shot out of a clump of undergrowth and, in a flash that I still can't measure, shoved my face down into the water. Then he pulled me up by my collar and propped me up against the grassy bank. For thirty seconds or so he made me watch his mouth as it chewed a large wad of gum. "I said watch," he threatened.

Like desks in a classroom, Eddie knew how gum worked, and I knew how he worked. He was chewing that gum for quite some time, opening and closing his mouth to let me see that there were other chewed things in the gum, things much more cruel than Saltines. Predictably now, he took the gum out of his mouth, held the horrible mass with the tips of his fingers—then slapped it, stretched it, and finally ground it into my head. "Do unto others what you do unto their brothers," he said. He disappeared over the other side of the creek. I got what I deserved, and I got off easier than I had feared, though I could smell something foul coming out of the gum. He kicked my crayfish jar across the stones; it broke open and the caught crustacean flipped backward in a straight line into the water.

So this was the world of revenge. Yup, Eddie transformed my head into the same life form that I had inflicted upon his little brother Joey's head; my life would now follow the same short-term trajectory: once again I would have to secretly steal into my mother's sewing cabinet and find the scissors, this time out of shame. Then I would have to take them to the bathroom, stand on the hamper, look at my own face in the bathroom mirror, and cut away Eddie's chewed gum. My head was going to look like hell.

Joey and I both received crew cuts and were labeled "the billiard brothers" around the neighborhood. This was a time for long hair, and it would take some time to grow back into that time. I got to the barber before Joey, but in the short period of time that Joey wore his hair with my haircut and before he became a billiard brother, he became somewhat of a sensation, especially at the Fergusonville community center, where there was a collective respect for Joey walking among them like that. Joey liked that attention, too, and after he had it all cut away and he joined the Society of the Crew-Cuts, he began to develop the annoying habit of constantly rubbing his own head and knocking on mine with his fist. I hated my head, especially the way the water would dry off it the minute I came out of the bath. It wasn't me, I didn't need a comb, and I didn't want rubbing. I prayed for a forgiving God to deliver me from my crew cut. "Please, God," I whispered to an ostensibly hippie deity, "make my hair grow and make things right."

Joey Helmuth went off to a public school in Croyden, and I was forced back to St. Thomas Aquinas with my green jacket and tie and my shaved head and my morning prayers. The kids at the bus stop had started in on me already, telling me I looked like a baby robin and making little peeping noises until I could get on. They threw stones at my Land of the Giants lunch box and broke the news to me that the show had been canceled. There's not too much that remains in memory after that. I guess my hair grew back on God's terms as I faded unnoticed into the backgrounds of hallways and formed other friendships that gave me a whole other set of stories, all of those things that take much longer than returning hair. Joey and I grew apart, the way things always happen when different schools and new friends enter the picture. After our family moved to Warminster two summers later, in fact, I never saw him again.

I saw a commercial for bubble gum the other night, and there were two kids in the scene sitting on the edge of a sandbox, chewing gum. I had the sound down because I was finishing a paper, and when I decided to take a break a little later in the night, I googled "Joey Helmuth" and I found this interesting story on a blog called musicianswheredidtheygo. com. It was an article posted by a guitarist from the late 70's whose name I had never heard, a fellow by the name of Whitey Plymouth. In the blog, Whitey was writing about a musician named Joe Helmuth from York, England:

"Joe Helmuth, the bass guitarist of the punk band The Skinwalkers, was found dead yesterday in a London hotel. He was 55. The Skinwalkers were a local London band that had brief success in the mid- seventies; they were actually quite good but were never in the right time and the right place to make it bigger, as is always the case with the luckless."

"I met Joe when he first arrived in York as a teenager and I can tell you God doesn't make humans any more the way He made Joe H. First and foremost, he could play most any instrument; I was enthralled with his cello and his harmonica routine was especially haunting. He only settled on bass because he wanted that sound; it was, as he put it, 'the force that glues the music.'"

"He was the soul of the Skinwalkers, even though he was not the lead singer and he didn't write any of their tunes. He had that wild hair, cut in all directions and all pink. Not much attention has been given to Joe's contribution to the start of the punk movement here in Britain, but I remember the day he arrived at my flat with that haircut and a new guitar, proclaiming that he had cut it himself. Then he got some pink dye and soaked his head in the sink, and he went out proudly to the clubs to play, and people took notice. Many people, pretty women, respected musicians, a newspaper that made fun, only gave him more positive attention. Pretty soon you saw bands with all sorts of bizarre hair styles, long after Joe had fallen by the wayside."

"Punk isn't around anymore, and way leads on to way, and someone like Joe with punked-out pink hair like that just doesn't stand out anymore. Maybe Joe's death had something to do with all that; they said heart attack, but it can't be that simple. Things and years came down between me and the Joe I knew, the Joe with an untaxed heart. For my money, Joe started the whole thing, I mean the WHOLE

THING. Music and hair styles as we know it today would not be possible without Joe Helmuth."

There were a handful of replies in the comments section of Whitey's blog, none of them noteworthy, except to reflect on the punk movement. None knew Joey, and I thought I might add something personal, you know, because of the gum thing and the amazing coincidence of pink. Maybe I might write something about fate and distance, and that it was definitely my best friend's heart that gave out, and that one night I googled and found him here on this blog just like that, and then end with something profound about shaved heads and changed lives and what does this discovery mean for me, for my life. But the blog was dated, the last comment made over a year ago, so I decided not to post because all that time and thought would consume me and get me away from my work, and no one would read it anyhow. What's the point of that?

EPIPHANY OF THE WISE MEN

THE MANGER SET in front of St. Thomas Aquinas church is now heavily chained down. Back in early January, someone stole the whole set, including Jesus, Mary, Joseph, the wise men statues, the hay, the entire hammered-together manger, the archangels, and the two spotlights suspended over baby Jesus, lights so bright that so that you could see Gabriel and Michael from the interstate. They must have unplugged the spotlights first and worked in the dark with at least two pick-ups, because that's what the tracks said.

Well into spring, everyone thought it was the Fitzsimmons kid; he fit the manger-stealing type (shaggy hair, godless eyes, etc.) and he had some room in a big shed in the back of his stepfather's yard besides. But Fitzsimmons was also a loner; he was weird because he sang to himself and no one wanted to be around him when he belted out showtunes. Further, he didn't have a pick-up, let alone helpers. Really though, none of us could quite imagine Fitzsimmons singing "Silent Night" or worse, some random showtune, to a Baby Jesus in a shed. Weird or not, he was just not that Christian, so probably not the thief, either.

Was there a market for mangers? for a life-sized ceramic Jesus baby? How about the six-foot tall wise men bearing gifts, what of those heavy plastered things? They had to weigh a hundred apiece. In some other part of the world, was this manger and the spotlights re-assembled for a bunch of people more Christian than us? But wait, how can they be more Christian than us if they steal, and steal religious artifacts to boot? What was the real God to think of those who stole His Baby Boy? This was some of the stuff we thought about sitting around Gus's Tavern. 'Weird" was what we would mutter over our cigarettes and our beer.

As summer dumped into fall, still no one knew who did it, and no one wanted to be held responsible for a second theft this time around, so they sent out a guy from Piedmont's with locks and chains to bolt down the Messiah and His Parents the first weekend in December. For nine straight hours the kid drilled holes and secured bolts and ran heavy chains through the holes to link the sheep, cows, and wise men, and then he dug two deep holes into the church-earth to moor Gabriel and Michael on thick wooden stakes. The spotlights were installed precariously on a ladder clearly too short (the kid had to stand on his tiptoes to drill), but the lights carried extra wattage this time so the lit-up manger could now be seen rounding the curve just past Exit 11.

No matter: pretty much nightly now that it has become December, we are waiting along the interstate with our weapons and our trucks for the spotlights on the archangels to go out. Someone's coming for sure; we know because we decided this at Gus's. We are certain, especially on account of our knowledge that other religious artifacts had been stolen from towns across the Midwest, with some south, and even a few manger scenes that disappeared from villages across central Europe. There was one town in South Dakota where the Virgin Mary statue had slipped off the back of a truck as it was being stolen, leaving it shattered at an intersection; several townspeople had to be moved to a psychiatric facility after seeing Mary's broken Smile and Her destroyed Appendages. There was another town somewhere south where they set fire to the remaining hay, and another where a Cabbage Patch doll was left in place of the Christ child. Mockery! We read the articles, saw the podcasts that offered theory after theory, and chatted in cyber-rooms about what to do to stop the manger-stealers this time around. It was cold, it was December, it was coming. We were comforted by the fact that it wasn't just us out here off the interstate as we drank and smoked some more. Groups just like ours were gathering across the country with a solidarity and a collective need to restore order. We are now connected by the internet and stationed everywhere. It is December and we are everywhere.

We don't know where you're taking our manger and our holy figures, you bastards, but we won't have it. No one steals Jesus, no one. We are the wiser men now, so fuck the gold, fuck the frankincense, and fuck the myrrh: we come bearing semi-automatic, bolt-action, and pump-action shotguns.

ASH FRIDAY

WHEN CARL WALKED out into the sandstorm, he did not know that he would never return. Instead, he thought that he might bring back his favorite cat Anson, who had once again escaped through the open door in search of some sort of freedom. Recanting the cat's name over and over into the blinding wind, Carl stepped cautiously into the storm and then thinned like a mirage until his wife, Ellie, standing at the door warning him to not venture too much further, watched herself become a widow.

The sandstorm, as wicked as they come to the Arizona desert, lasted four days and five nights, by which time Carl had tried to find his way back and died of thirst three hundred yards from his doorstep and three hundred two yards from his water faucet—the way it always happens. When his wife found him, his mouth was filled with sand and his eyes had discolored to a pale yellow. Carl's hands, which had begun to stiffen, seemed to be clawing the now-tranquil air, as if, in his last moments of existence, he could not tell ground from sky.

On the Friday following his death, Ellie had Carl cremated and placed into an urn on the pie table. She explained to her nearest neighbors, two miles down Hatch Road, that Carl had requested in a will that he spend eternity as ash. "Right in the middle of his custom living room is the place for him," she said, "Right in the middle of what he carved with mortal hands."

Ellie was seven months pregnant when her husband died, so she had to make all of the preparations for delivery herself. She and Carl had already begun to fix up the extra room. After Carl's death, though, she had to assemble the crib without instructions, which took her several days and created a distinctive scar on her left hand where the screwdriver had slipped. When the contractions got to twenty minutes apart, she got on her husband's old Harley, the way he'd instructed her to at the picnic, and drove herself into Tucson. The doctor, upon finding out how she came to the hospital, lectured her about the dangers of driving a motorcycle while in labor, though he could not immediately recall any evidence to support his claim. The birth came without incident. She could not think of a name for her child and why did the son of a bitch have to go out for the cat? After the boy lay in a bassinet for two full days, she decided on Sandy. She knew the name would probably be construed as a cruel joke, not because Sandy was more of a girl's name, but because of the manner in which her husband Carl had died. But she liked the name because it was her best friend's name back in Philadelphia, and so she printed it on the certificate and that was that.

Living in the ranch off Highway 43, miles distant from neighbors and the rain and the world of fathers, Sandy grew old enough to learn the dangers of sandstorms. His mother Ellie sat him down at the dinner table one windy evening and told him of the unfortunate event that had made her life a veritable hell. "You get lost ten yards from the house," she said. "A cat isn't worth a human life," she said. "The desert is a mighty cruel place," she said. "I wish your father could be here for you," she said.

After some tears, Sandy and his mother flipped through an old photo album. *Who are the two figures walking in azalea parks and at the edges of oceans and sitting under Christmas trees and walking down streets in big cities?*

Sandy came to discover, or more precisely he was told, that they were his mother and father.

"That's you? That's you?" he squealed.

His mother smiled sickly and explained about what makes people age besides time. Her hair didn't stay combed and atop her head anymore and it wasn't jet black and her face wasn't nearly as thin, and she certainly didn't smile like that now. Sandy shivered at that smile because how could the woman in that photograph and the woman breathing next to him be the same person? He didn't remember ever seeing the breathing woman smile. "The desert heat and the dirt and the long nights, they do something to make you look very different," was what she told him. "I lose sleep when the wind comes up and the sand hits the side of the house and before I know it daylight comes and I can't recover. I can't recover."

Sandy asked his mother about the man. He kept saying 'the man' because he couldn't seem to say *father* in order to make that image come off the page and breathe. He was old enough at seven, but he felt a tugging inside him that kept *father* off his lips.

His mother told him how she and the man had moved to Arizona from Philadelphia, a place where ice forms and snow falls and sandstorms don't exist and people gather by the hundreds of thousands to go to things like plays and baseball games and fancy restaurants. "And they live on top of one another," she said, and that made Sandy really think and ask questions about high-rises lost in the mist and long elevator rides to the very tops of the world.

"Your father always wanted to go back," she said. "He talked about the baseball fields on Ellsworth and his best friend JoJo Culp and the trolley stops by the sounds of the bell." Then his mother began to mumble, the vague way he remembered mumbling himself before he could find the words to talk.

Sandy was left alone at the dinner table with only those images, and he flipped forward and backward and felt the cool breeze from the turn of every cardboard page. On one of the last pages of that photo album, he ran his fingers around a picture of the man alone in a corner booth as if he were a map, and he breathed close against the plastic and tried to make him come to life.

Later, his mother put the album away at the top of her closet to make room for dinner at the table and to once again cover memories with layers of dust. Sandy ate his pea soup, broke his crackers on the surface, and made a mental note of where she put the album. He was going to get up there and get it, look at it again when she went out in the truck to get more groceries or when she fell asleep to the evening news. He thought about stealing a couple of the photographs and putting them beneath his pillow. He kept thinking of the man in the corner booth. The man had finished a plate of something and was staring ahead as if he were waiting for some dessert.

Sandy thought about his father's eyes, trying to come off the page, as his mother served him strawberry ice cream.

Just after Sandy turned fourteen, he sat down beneath a tall cactus with Robbie Hurst and drank a wine-sack of blackberry brandy. The sun had just set, and he could hear the distant howls of a pack of coyotes massing for their night hunt. The first time they had drunk from the sack, three weeks back, Sandy wound up getting sick all over the desert floor, so this time he was going to pace himself. Robbie was three years older than Sandy and his father let him drink, so he could polish off a whole sack himself. Robbie had lost his hand in a 'kitchen accident' with his father. Accident was the way Robbie described it, but Sandy's mother had told him different. She had told him that his drunken father had cut it off with a weed-whacker. When Sandy had enough alcohol in him, and when the night insects came up to drown out his voice from possibly carrying down to Highway 43, he asked Robbie about the stump.

"I told you kitchen accident," was all Robbie said and then a swig.

"Well my mom says your dad did it with a weed whacker," Sandy said.

Robbie got up off his boulder and said, "Well what the fuck does your mother know?" and tossed a stone into the darkness with his lone hand and said, "At least if my old man died, my mom wouldn't keep his ashes in an urn in the middle of a table."

"What do you mean ashes-table-old man?" Sandy asked all in a row.

Then just the howling coyotes came, and Robbie wanted to change the subject, got suddenly quiet, went off into the dark, and pissed on a cactus.

"What do you mean, ashes?"

"My mother told me that your mother had your father cremated and she keeps him on some special pie table or something."

Sandy remembered the mumbles that often came from the living room in the middle of the night, and how he had witnessed, on several occasions, what seemed to be his mother talking to a vase. Earlier in his life, he thought that a genie had been trapped in there, or that his mother was going crazy from the desert heat and that some sort of fever would just overcome her at times because of that heat. Now, as he sat on his rock and stared off in the direction of the massing coyotes, he remembered the photo album he had never bothered to get down from the top of the closet seven years back. It was behind the shoe boxes.

Sandy's mother slept on the couch and let the television put her to sleep. She had done this for so long that she couldn't get to sleep any other way. It was only when the mindlessness of late- night talk shows would settle into her brain that she would tire and drift off. Sandy estimated that his mother had not slept in the big double bed in the back bedroom, her bedroom, in his lifetime. He felt the chill more each day as he looked into a room, unlived in and forgotten, that had become an unspoken shrine to her dearly departed Carl. In all his years, Sandy had never stepped foot beyond the doorway barrier of that ghostly room.

Dizzy from the brandy, Sandy stood on a chair and reached into the back of the closet shelf. There he found it, exactly where it had been left seven years before. In the dim light of the hallway, he propped the album up against the yellowed wall, watched the dust drop from its cover and leafed through the photographs.

A father I got a father here he is and here he is and here and over here and on every single page. His face, his eyes, his legs in jeans. Does he look like me? Do I look like him? There he is among the azaleas, there he is at the edge of the water, there he is up against a brick wall and standing over a grate, there he is sitting on a long wall and there he is, all alone, sitting in a corner booth.

Sandy turned and looked into the living room glowing with television light.

There he is on the table right in the middle of that pie table. My mother burned him to ash and now she has made him a god. She kneels before his altar and wishes his soul well. She speaks to him in whispers and thinks I cannot hear. She sleeps next to him there on the couch and lets the television light bathe her to sleep and she doesn't tell me a thing.

Sandy removed his sneakers in the hallway so as not to make any noise and walked across the living room tile. He picked up the urn, held his father in the palms of his hands, gripping him tightly. His mother turned and yawned, then fell back into her deep sleep.

Why didn't she tell me? My father is ash but why didn't she tell me? He was here all the time, right in front of me. I grew up with him all around me and never knew it. Why didn't she tell me?

He shook the ashes and they felt like sand. His father died in sand, and now he felt like sand. Sandy remembered Philadelphia and Ellsworth Street and his mother telling him seven years ago, right in the other room at the kitchen table, how his father wanted so much to go back.

What if there could be a genie?" What if my mother could summon a genie to take the man back home? That would have been one of her three wishes if there could be a genie: she would wish that he could just go back to the baseball fields of Ellsworth. Why are you out here anyway? What brought you out here from that other place, from that Philadelphia?

In the dim light of the hallway, Sandy took the urn and put it under his arm. He walked into the back room for the first time in his life and clicked on the light. He crossed the chilly threshold and looked at the bed. It was still made from fourteen years ago, with a flowery quilt of vines and purple flowers that gently touched the floor. Perhaps she had slept in it once or twice since his father had disappeared into the storm. But then, when the nights turned painfully restless and the wind haunted the sides of the house, she came out into the living room to stay with her companion the television. There were some of Sandy's baby pictures on the wall and a big picture of a grassy field over the bed. There was a black cross between the windows with no Jesus at all. There was a hairbrush, some makeup, his mother's pocketbook on the dresser. The mirror was coated with a yellow film.

He put his father down on the bed. He rested him there and looked at the urn, half expecting something to happen. His mother rustled in the other room. She would not awaken, he knew that. The television whispered some commercials. Sandy took his mother's pocketbook and sat down on the edge of the bed, rustling through it. He found two hundred dollars in twenties and some change in the side pocket. Then he found, hooked to the side of her purse, the keys to the truck. Robbie had taught himself how to drive his father's Impala through the desert, around the cactuses like a serpentine course while churning up desert dust, and even a little down 43 when the coast was clear of oncoming headlights, usually just before dawn and usually after some brandy.

Sandy had sat in his mother's pick-up truck many times. He had played with the shifter and held the steering wheel, so he was ready to take it down the highway and into town now. He would need to worry about red lights, about traffic and four-way stop signs and then open highway when the time came. But first he would need to get a map. If he wanted to go all the way east, all the way back to Philadelphia, he was going to need a map.

Sandy picked up the urn and left the house. With two hundred dollars, on a meal a day and with a little luck, he could make it east and back. In the dark, with the night insects converging and the light from the television coming through the open screen, he sat in the truck and wondered why. On the seat were the ashes of a man he had never met except through the pages of a photo album. Why didn't he just wake his mother and tell her his plan? Surely, she would say good idea and take the ashes there herself. Surely, she would want to go back there again. Why should he risk all of this at fourteen, without a license and a reason at all? Perhaps the brandy was talking. He felt the dizziness in his brain, but nevertheless he slid the keys into the ignition and started up the truck. *The engine will not wake her. She sleeps like a stone through the talk shows.*

Sandy thought of the photograph of the man in the comer booth again. He pondered it in much the same way he had pondered it when he was seven. His father was alone in a corner booth waiting for the dessert, so Sandy reasoned, from whatever he interpreted from that image, that he must do this thing alone. This moment in time was his corner booth, so he must carry on alone.

He shifted quickly into drive, covering several hundred yards before turning on the lights. In that time, in the utter darkness, he had gone off the road and through some shrub. He got back on the highway and checked in the mirror to see if his mother might be running down the middle of 43 waving her arms and screaming his name above the buzzing insects.

No, not my mother. She will sleep until dawn, until I am gone from Arizona and out of the west

With the map of the country unfolded beside him on the seat, Sandy reminded himself to stop somewhere in east Texas to drop some change into a phone booth and call his mother and then he remembered. Ellsworth Street, his mission. From the Texas phone call, he projected his path forward, out of the great desert and out of all that he had ever known, through the towns one by one, following the red veins of the map until he was over the vast Mississippi. The endless highways, the rise of so many tall buildings, the congestion of so many people, one on top of the other. The heat would be gone, the cold would come, and the ice would hang in the air like a benediction. He would get to Philadelphia by Friday morning. Then he would search the long, intricate maze of streets that would lead him deeper and deeper into a new world, lost and lost and lost again until he finally found that street called Ellsworth.

In downtown Tucson Sandy caught himself, in the rear-view mirror, smiling at the red light.

On Friday afternoon I will lift the urn of my father high over my head and the wind will surely come up. I will watch his ashes drift out over the baseball fields. Some of the ash will fall to the fields, some of the ash will settle into my hair, some of the ash will become one with the city.

THE CAR FELL ON RICKY'S FLAT TOE*

IN WHISPER DOWN the Lane once, I started with the sentence "the car fell on Ricky's flat toe," hoping it wouldn't morph into a pile of words. Rodgie Butterworth, Ricky's younger brother and seven years old, was at the end of the lane of eight because he was late and because he was little. I wanted my whispered sentence to arrive at him intact, for I knew Rodgie would get angry and quit because he adored his brother Ricky, because he was always at the end, and because it was fun to make him mad and walk away. Rodgie, you see, needed to grow up some more, and this was me helping him.

The sentence arrived intact and Rodgie walked away. This time, however, Rodgie became extra angry. It was as intense an anger as I have ever seen in someone seven, the flush red on his face telling us that he had had enough, and then the insane stomping of his feet the length of the sidewalk home, as if this mockery of his perfect older brother Ricky was the breaking point. In fact, Rodgie never played Whisper Down the Lane with us again.

Then, the following summer, he lit the schoolyard on fire with his mother's matches, pummeled the sliding board with his father's hammer, urinated and shat in the sandbox like his cat, and graduated finally in September to stealing Jerry Robinson's bike, and just after Jerry had gotten it for his birthday! When he was punished by his parents by having to stay in his room, Rodgie solved that problem by opening the window and running away from home. They found him two days later behind the makeshift bar in the Devoe's basement, where he had subsisted on a stash of warm bottled water and Ritz crackers. After that, Rodgie drifted away across the Benson Creek bridge and into the company of the Newportville delinquents.

Years later, after I moved away to Bolrath, grew up, married, and had a mortgage and children, and with some extra time one night, I performed a google search for "Roger Butterworth" and I discovered where he was today: PRISON.

*Be careful what you whisper.

Y

THE FETUS-FINGER was mistaken for a penis on the ultrasound, so Ted jumped the gun, went out to the Wal-Mart, and decorated his soon-to-be-baby-boy's bedroom with baseballs and footballs and posters and deep blue paint. Then, mostly at night before he fell asleep during the last months of Macy's surprising and miraculous pregnancy, Ted planned the long expanse of his boy's childhood, of being his son's sports coach all along the way, under which he would build the shelves to hold all of his trophies and fit the frames with photos and articles of his boy's heroic moments. Baseball or football? Ice hockey or basketball? Wrestling? It didn't matter. Sports was sports, and there would be articles and trophies from those sports to put up on walls. Mostly, though, he could tell the stories of his heroes to his son: the great Joe Montana, the humble Barry Sanders, the unbelievable Jerry Rice, the puzzling but talented Richie Allen.

The fetus of course emerged a girl, and Ted's dream of coaching a son was dashed. His wife Macy was adamant that there would be no more attempts at a child because this difficult pregnancy was sheer hell, and a hell to never be revisited. One was enough and one more than I really wanted anyway, she confessed. But she smiled and held the baby and agreed to name her Billie, because that was the name Ted had picked out while he dreamed of a boy athlete.

Macy had played soccer in high school, so, in the first months of parenthood, she tried to talk to Ted about girl sports, that they too were worth playing and paying attention to, but he would have none of it. He was not going to coach a bunch of girls or research the great women players so he could talk her to his little girl about them, nor would he be inspired, if she did decide on a sport, to build shelves that would hold cheerleading and field hockey trophies. No, this has not been my hope since that damned ultrasound mistook a finger for a penis.

The day after they brought Billie home, Macy took down the Joe Montana and Barry Sanders posters from above the crib, the signed footballs and the Cole Hamels bobblehead from atop the shelf, and talked to Ted about the beginning path of their baby girl's life. In the ensuing weeks, and with the feigned consent of her husband, Macy constructed a wall of photos depicting baby mammals, the Pacific Ocean at dawn, and colored drawings of multicultural children running through fields of daffodils. She wanted to turn the room pink, or at least a pale shade of yellow, but she wouldn't push Ted that far. Later in the week, Ted took the Barry Sanders poster rolled up behind the couch and fastened it to one of his office walls.

Ted agreed with Macy and didn't want any more children after that. One was enough, children were massively expensive, and he didn't want to take the chance that he would need to raise two girls besides. He wanted a boy on the first shot, and he wanted to name him Billy, and he wanted him to play sports. Now, even with the minor consolation of calling his girl Billie with an E, he had nevertheless lost the Y. Now every time he saw his daughter's name in print, he would realize that he had conceded the Y, conceded a son who would tear up the league and settled for Billie with an E instead. He would never ever admit it, especially to his daughter, but it was settling.

"In another life I might have been a player, a great player," Ted told Ruth in the night. "I wish I had the confidence to try out for the baseball team, but my eyesight was not good and I couldn't catch fly balls in the outfield and I didn't know that all I needed was glasses until it was too late. I didn't know, my mother and father didn't know, until it was too late. If I had just had glasses early on and I could see the ball coming, who knows?"

Macy sighed and turned. It was the same story all through her pregnancy, even before the pregnancy.

"And I was too small growing up and all I wanted to do was play football. It was my only fantasy. I wanted to be a fast running back and score touchdowns, that was my fantasy...the new kid, the fast new running back when we moved to Fergusonville....I tried out for the team but I was twelve and you had to register for the 115-pound team if you were twelve, and I only weighed 65 pounds. Sixty-five. The coach talked my father out of letting me sign, and on the way out I dropped my application in the trash can and deferred to joining the Boy Scouts."

Macy was waiting for the part of the story that always came next, of the five-year-old Ted in his white helmet with the wings drawn on, looking at himself in the mirror, mimicking an NFL announcer, and saying his name: "For the Philadelphia Eagles.... running back Ted Sullivan.... weighing forty-five pounds..." as he fantasized entering the field of play, while his mother watched him from the hall, and then, a thousand times over during his manhood and marriage, his mother telling Macy the story with the same inevitable cackle, about how cute he looked standing on the bed with that oversized helmet and looking at himself in the mirror. But Ted didn't mention the mirror or his mother this time. Instead, he turned silently with his pillows in the middle of his story and snapped off the light. Later, as Macy was drifting off to sleep, she could distinctly hear her husband sobbing.

WHEN BILLIE TURNED nine, Ted came around. Billie had practiced hard and won the position of center for the Fergusonville soccer team. Though he was proud of her, Ted had maintained his disinterest through all of it, a defiant stubbornness through the cheerleading, through the softball, and now the early days of the soccer. That task fell on Macy, who took her to practices and games and then filled Ted in at the dinner table on what she had done. Ted went to the games when he could. He had always made sure his job as an accountant kept him busy, even when it wasn't tax season, for to get too invested in his daughters' exploits on the field would certainly make him feel the pangs of regret for not having a boy again, for the male product of his own flesh running for touchdowns or catching deep fly balls up against fences, for a boy about to become a man hoisting trophies that he had once imagined so clearly in his head for his sixty-five pound self, except now, he wanted to see his son in that mirror. It's what he had always wanted.

One day, Ted came home with a massive headache after a marathon of tax returns. It was early April, in the insane torrent of tax season, and he didn't know how many more tax seasons he could go on, as his temple pounded and he squinted at the ceiling, closing his eyes finally for some small relief. There would be twenty-hour days immediately ahead, ones in which he would take naps on the office futon, drowned in numbers, as he gave his body rest between the piles of returns. It would go on and on, January to April, for the rest of his life, or at least until he reached the abyss of retirement. Just numbers, but only numbers, he considered as his head raged. This is my legacy now.

Eyes still closed, Ted listened to the conversation between Billie and Macy at the kitchen table, as his wife talked of the great women soccer players. Marta from Brazil, Sun Wen from China, Hope Solo, Abby Wambach, and Michelle Akers from the USA. Ruth stopped and weighed in more heavily on Mia Hamm. "Mia was a military brat, traveling and moving, traveling and moving, never permanence.....one of her biggest heroes that sustained her through all of that was Wayne Gretzky."

Ted listened up; his head cleared a bit as he opened his eyes. Gretzky was The Great One.

"Mia's biggest hero was her older brother Garrett, who died of a rare bone disease when Mia was a young lady," Macy went on. "Her favorite person in the world, dead just like that. She lost her brother and she cried, but she also tried. She tried so much that she became a champion soccer player. Mia played on the U.S. women's national soccer team for seventeen years. Mia won the Women's World Cup in 1991 and 1999. Mia took Olympic gold medals in 1996 and 2004. Mia is one of my favorites."

That Christmas, after a long uneventful summer and fall following what was a particularly horrendous tax season (what with the new codes), Ted ordered three posters off Amazon--one for his office and two for Billie's room. He ordered The Great One for his office, a marvelous photo showing Gretsky's patented slap-shot when he played for the Edmonton Oilers, and for Billie he bought a poster of Mia Hamm and another of her teammate Brandi Chastain. On that poster, under the caption World Cup

Champions, Brandi Chastain was on her knees and held the unmistakable face of victory, along with her own shirt gripped in her left fist. She had taken the shirt off after the penalty kick went through, which he so remembered from watching the game. On the poster, blown up to three feet tall, she wore only her sports bra, because the women's team had just won the World Cup on her penalty kick, and because she could just wear a sports bra now and nobody was ever going to say anything except good.

Ted was going to wait until she opened her present and, after Billie unrolled the poster, he would tell her Brandi Chastain's story, a story he had memorized just for this Christmas morning moment: "Billie, Brandi wasn't even on the top five to kick. She had missed a heartbreaking penalty kick off the crossbar against China four months earlier and her coach demoted her. So Brandi switched her penalty kicks to her left foot as a way to fool the goalkeepers. Her coach Tony DiCicco, perhaps sensing something about her, bumped her up on the list to the fifth spot."

Ted lay in bed on Christmas Eve and recited the rest in his head, energized about the new sports information he had learned, forgetting now the torrential tax season about to arrive. "With nine kicks down, Chastain went up to the box with her chance to win it. She used her left foot and watched the ball sail past the surprised Chinese goalkeeper for the win. The country celebrated."

Macy knew her husband well enough to know that when he had trouble sleeping, sometimes it was because he felt regret about what might have been in his life and that sometimes he cried to himself on those regrets, he just a forgettable accountant in a sea of forgettable accountants. But she also knew he lost sleep when he was excited, and on this night, on this Christmas Eve in particular, he was clearly excited as he waited restless for the morning light. It was Christmas the next day, and he was going to get up and give Billie the posters. Macy knew somehow that his excitement would not end there. In the morning after the presents were unwrapped, after coffee, or at some moment in the coming week perhaps, Ted would express his interest in coaching soccer for Billie's team. He was going to want a whistle and a clipboard, and he was going to want to stand on the sidelines so that he could watch every moment of her footwork.

PULU SI BAGOOMBA

ON MOST MORNINGS, he would kill the silence by pressing the crunch button. The loud grinding noise of the compactor had whittled away at his eardrums over the years and left him partly deaf. When he started hanging off garbage trucks years ago, the thing that mattered to him most was how many people was he going to wake up, and could he dump softly. But, eventually, he gave in to Willie and Sash, who had grown careless of the sleepers. They had grown tired of their own cautious footsteps and whispered directions and listening to each other's voices drown beneath the crunching. No, they told Spookytooth, you have to shout and rise above the noise. So what if you wake them, they told him. They'll all be getting up to their noisy clocks anyway, and why should we suffer?

They named him Spookytooth on the second day. He had just visited a dentist who installed, at the tip of one of his incisors, a temporary bond that turned out to be phosphorescent, and, for the two-week interval between visits, his mouth glowed in the dark. From the opposite side of the truck and in the morning darkness, when it was blue but mostly black, Willie and Sash said they saw the dark shadow of their new co-worker moving over to the curb and back with a little glow in the middle of his face. Sash said he would "eyeball the star" as it whispered across his mirror and crept back to the truck.

At the bottom of Lincoln Drive and across the silent ocean of sleeping houses, he heaved the metal can toward the curb with a snap of his forearms. He turned back for the slippery rusting handle just above his shoulder and anticipated the crash of the can and the lights that might flick on somewhere nearby. "Let's get a move on, a get-go" he shouted out to the morning. His body lurched as the truck pulled ahead and he dragged his toe heels across the moving street and over the glistening of several spilled sandwich bags.

Seventeen years he counted as he picked up 43 Elsie. Seventeen years and six months come Sunday since he walked into the inner office and applied for the job. Twelve years since Eddie left, two years the last he heard from him. Eleven since they ripped down the mall after the shooting to put up electrical coils and six and a half since they fired Neal when he took the teenager home. His memories were merely islands now, foggy patches of rock thousands of miles apart, and here he was, sailing and waiting for the next good one.

Spooky could tell from across the wet black lawn there'd been hell last night in 43 Elsie. The bedroom curtains were drawn and there was another broken window in the room above the garage. They'd lost their twist ties again, too. He could hear the muffled echo of some shouts from the back kitchen and the faint dropping of what sounded like a heavy appliance. Spooky remembered the dog accident just at the end of their driveway two years back—the poor lady who sat drunk in a sweat suit on the boulder as he lifted her cans. She was crying with her drink tipped at 5 a.m., staring at the dark stain on the blacktop as if it had just happened, muttering to herself 'my baby was alive just a minute ago' and hoping that the trash men might solve her problem. Some drunken visitor must have backed over her dog, that's what he remembered thinking anyway, some stranger that just came and drank her alcohol and staggered to his van and then crushed her Yorkie with his back tire. He figured that she was going to stay there on the rock staring a while longer next to her empty cans to think about things, all drunk and pie-eyed and searching in the shrubs for the answer.

Something somewhere was going to give at 43 Elsie; Spooky could just feel their tension in their bags. He heaved their load into the back, watching one of the bags burst open, spilling two empty cans of solid white tuna out the edge of the truck. She had got it on sale, he thought as a can rolled over his shoe: normally there were cans of Chunk Light in her garbage. The guy he heard yelling from the back room and punching the paneling probably hated solid white tuna. There was a little trail of tall grass along the edge of the sidewalk leading to the door. The guy had done a poor job cutting, and she probably let him know about it while he was drunk off the football game. Or maybe the mower was old.

Somewhere something clicked in the part of Spookytooth's brain that could make him predict short-term futures (that was why he did little stock market ventures and football pools on the side). He saw the next trash pick-up at 43 Elsie like the next logical step in a series of algebraic variables: there was going to be blood on something that someone dumped in the trash, dried up perhaps in clumps of cheap paper towels and stuffed carelessly near the top. Nobody would be home and he pictured their minivan gone. Yes, he thought, someone somewhere would have to die at the end of this equation.

The grind of the motor into drive beckoned him to the handle as he glanced ahead at 45. He felt the dew dangling from his shirt. It chilled him, though nothing like the sweat later on as the sun came up and the smell began to rise. The ones in 45 are restaurant people, Sash told him. The son took over the house after his father had moved out with Greenpeace and left the eighteen-year-old his house and his bank account, a good luck note with a P.S. that condemned capitalism, and a twenty dollar bill with a hammer and sickle buried in Hamilton's head. Or at least that's the way Sash remembered hearing it.

"Yep," Sash said in the morning blue, "Guy in maintenance told me the kid got himself a waiter job at The Twisted Vine Veranda and brings all his other waitbuddies over every single night. And the son of a bitches must be makin' some damn good tip money." He lifted a Cinch-Sack full of clinking bottles and the bag glistened with wet, stale beer. "Damn if every one of these clinking here isn't imported."

Spooky thought Sash an okay co-worker most of the time, except when he would go to sleep on the passenger side. That was when Willie would have to shove him hard against the door to wake him. While he was driving along, Willie would curse Sash in his high-pitched shouts to get to the back of the truck and slap him around with his right hand. "Wake the fuck up," his demand would burst out on open bedroom windows. Sleeping families must have thought he was speaking to them.

Spooky remembered the verbal lashing Corky the district supervisor had given Sash in the lot one Friday afternoon about the complaints he was receiving. "What the hell is going on?" Corky asked. "We've gotten a couple of angry calls about dirty-mouthed trash men and a serious letter about someone slamming cans and using the f word all the way up the street."

Sash never admitted to acting that way. "We're almost quieter than church mice," he fibbed.

Besides those calls and that single letter, no one else had ever complained of Willie and Sash's weekly ritual. With each loud outburst, Spooky imagined all the listeners lying awake in their beds, angry and under control for years, tired men and women staring at their ceilings, some of them a razor-line away from shouting out the window. He could just feel their mental anguishes hanging in the air with the dew. It was only a matter of time before there came stamps across the wet grass in bare toes and bathrobes and raised voices. Today might be the day the fellow over at 77 Sullivan comes out and clenches his fists, Spooky thought. Or the big-game hunter over on Wellsley might advance on us with his moose rifle.

Sash stayed up nights and watched his Gilligan's Island videos. When he wasn't asleep on the passenger side or whispering about the houses and the people beneath their roofs, he was talking about some episode of Gilligan and hitting Spooky on the head with his cap, just like Skipper.

"Damn if that one when they turn into chicken people isn't funny... you know, the one where the Mars probe accidentally lands on the island and the space guys in Florida think it's on Mars because Gilligan put the lid on the pot of glue?... it blew up and got on everybody and they were so pissed they chased Gilligan into a feather hut and all got a million feathers on them so they looked like birds and they ran in front of the camera when the Florida guys turned it on and the stupid Florida guys thought they were watching Martians and the castaways didn't get rescued." Sash whistled a couple notes of the theme song. "Yep, they sure were pissed at Gilligan."

Sometimes Spooky would interrupt him, and tell Sash he'd heard that particular episode a thousand times too many, like the ones Sash called favorites, when Maryann thought she was Ginger or when the Kincaid guy hunted Gilligan or when they all ate the mind-reading seeds off the mysterious bush. He'd ask Sash if there was something else he could talk about because it was such a ridiculous show and how they didn't have energizer batteries for radios back then or Republicans going out to sea with Democrats running the boat and who were they fooling with their three-hour tour. But that would always make Sash throw the cans harder and talk louder and wake more people, so Spooky would usually listen and take it, anticipating Sash's words and tone as he replayed the memory of a just-watched episode.

Over at 66 Omega, they'd just sprung for new cans. New cans were nice because they were easy to spot with their shiny aluminum glow, and they were lighter because they weren't weighed down by the heavy crust of years of leaking milk and rotted fruit. They smelled like freshly stamped metal; there was no sourness here. As Spooky picked them up, they reminded him of his years at Standard Pressed Steel when he was grinding away at the lathe; the boys would all punch out at three and dash across the boulevard to play baseball and drink beer. He used to catch, and he squatted in the dirt with the mitt his father had given him from when he played with the Senators. He called the pitches, too, even though it was only softball and the choices were either underhand or overhand. He'd keep his plastic cup of beer right there in the dirt, and he'd have to quick pick it up if the batter got a hit and somebody rounded third and he'd guzzle it if he knew there was going to be a play at the plate. He remembered the boss suspended him because Spooky had tagged him out at home, though Mr. Burton used the excuse that Spooky hadn't recalibrated the lathe the next day and he had had enough of the misfired hex nuts.

That was when Spooky owned the duplex out in Fergusonville and lifted weights, when he had the bushy moustache and a blonde wife and he was taking in forty grand from the job and selling water purifiers on the weekends. That was when he had the tenants below him dealing drugs at all hours, heroine and cocaine stashed behind the cabinets he'd installed, and he didn't know about the drugs until the FBI came swarming up his driveway in black cars and holsters filled with loaded guns. He could still hear the echo from the megaphone, ordering him and his wife to the floor and calling for the criminals to come out, and then the scuffle of feet from outside the windows, tackling and yelling obscenities as his tenants were hauled away. The arrest was on the front page of the paper the next day, a picture of his duplex in the background with the handcuffed boys brushing past the camera, and the little quote his wife had given the reporter, "We were harboring criminals and didn't have a clue."

Mr. Burton called him into the office and slid the newspaper forward, with red ink circled around the words "works at Standard Pressed Steel." Burton told Spooky, "I've had about enough of you disgracing the name of this company, and your consistent errors and your talk about unionizing and this especially, living with felons... I'm afraid I'm going to have to let you go."

So he moved on, and found no luck in securing another factory job, finally applying to the sanitation company and settling for the offer of second shift. His hours were now opposite his wife's, and he'd leave the house at midnight and get home in late morning, sleeping through the afternoon and part of the evening. Most of the time he'd come home tired and smelly, and his wife began to complain about the clothes she'd have to wash and the way they left all the others with a stench. She'd insisted he find something with better hours and a more pleasant odor because she couldn't take him laying asleep on the couch all the way through the evening news with no one to talk to, always eating alone and keeping the leftovers warm. "Besides that, I've got a closet full of dresses that reek of old garbage," she said.

Spooky had lost his sense of smell as the years went by, and now his hearing began to go. He couldn't find another factory job, and eventually had given up trying, given up losing sleep to go out in the afternoons to look for something better. He had filled out applications across town and wore suits to interviews, flossing his teeth and smiling, but to no avail. His blonde wife had begun to see another man, the cashier over at Flash-Mart that always wore the bow tie. Then she cleaned out the bedroom closet and left one morning, when Spooky had just fallen asleep under the fan. He'd found her apologetic note tacked on the refrigerator, wishing him the best. He sold his duplex at a loss several months after her departure and moved closer to the sanitation plant.

Spooky picked up the load of the widow at 66 Omega, two large trash bags stuffed to capacity. He felt the bottom of the bags begin to give and he quickly swung them in a circle around his back and heaved them into the air and toward the truck. They tore apart as they settled into the back, spilling the guts of a renovated room, old wallpaper and plaster and crusted newspaper. He looked at the front of the house as he crunched her debris. Judging by the knick-knacks in her picture window, she was a neat freak. It seemed to Spooky as if every alabaster figure on the ledge had been measured and placed at the same distance from the next figure. The arms and legs conspired in the same direction like Rockettes, shiny and polished and at equal distances, their little beady black eyes all lined up and looking at you as you advanced up the walk, guarding things almost.

Behind her drawn curtains, the living room had to be spotless, and you could probably catch the odor of Boysenberry before you walked in the door, and there were probably cut lilies in the foyer and copies of Architectural Digest fanned out on her Butler table. She had a fish tank with an aquatic frog, or a wall of awards from some long-gone son for amateur wrestling, or an Executive-of-the-Year award from her dead husband's job. She had furry slippers and drank her tea out of little porcelain cups that could pass for a dollhouse set, except the china was imported from England and you had to wash it in room temperature water or it would shatter. Spooky remembered the empty cardboard case of Darjeeling one trash day and he thought she must be addicted to the stuff to buy it in bulk supply like that. Or maybe it was just a moving box.

Sash was loud again this week, mostly because Willie had badgered him about the palm trees; how four able-bodied men couldn't fashion some sort of boat out of logs to take them off the island was beyond him. If all the dumb natives that showed up in canoes could do it, why couldn't some big seaman, an intellectual professor, and a capitalist pig? Sash started cursing and tossing cans high in the air and made them crash louder as he tried to defend the Skipper, the professor, and Mister Howell.

"You idiot! Can't you see if they get off the island the whole series would be over?"

Sash started talking about Edgar, his old co-worker, the one he referred to as *The Philosopher*. "Now he used to listen *with respect* to my Gilligan stories," he said. "He'd listen and then he would talk about being trapped... you know, how Gilligan always screwed things up so they never got rescued and how maybe it was a voice coming out of Gilligan's head telling him he really didn't want to be rescued, to stay in the misery of his island with a fat guy forever beating on him."

Sash glared at Willie's reflection in the mirror.

"Yeah, Edgar used to tell me Gilligan wasn't just Gilligan, but a symbol for every human being — we are all stuck on islands just like his and trapped by a fear, a fear of change, a fear that things might get worse. 'Better to be familiar with misery', Edgar used to say all the time. 'When the time comes,' he used to say, 'we all lock ourselves in caves just as the rescue plane flies over.'" Then, as Sash grabbed hold of the handle, "God, I miss Edgar."

Spooky saw the truck turn up Marshall to 65 to the house with the dirt lawn and the beige shutters. He noticed the boy coming out of the hedges just then, pushing along in his big wheel in only a pair of stained underpants. The doors were shut, that's what Spooky noticed, the front door was closed shut as this two-year-old kid made his way up the driveway all glassy-eyed in his underwear, turning his wheel into the stones and dragging his bare toes across the cement, slurring out long unintelligible words that Spooky translated to "I want to come inside". The pity Spooky felt just then was unlike any other pity, an empty churning in his stomach he hadn't had since those sleepless nights after his wife took off with the bow-tied cashier.

Willie whispered as he picked up their cans, "The mother got taken away for stealing evening dresses from K-Mart a month back...it was her tenth shoplifting offense and while she was in overnight, in a cell with a bunch of animal-rights activists, she unthinkingly squashed a roach with her heel as it tried to run past her...before she knew it they were on her, that pack of animal-rights activists, clawing and scratching the way angry ladies do, screaming 'lousy murderer' and slamming her head against the bars, all the while screaming about bug feelings and who the hell are you."

Willie and Spooky watched as the little boy tried to look in the misted windows, dropping the stones from his hands, cooing like a hungry pigeon. But the house was shut tight as a drum. The truck moved on.

Spooky was quietly listening today, as Sash arrived to the subject of Gilligan. Sash recounted the totem pole episode, another one Spooky had heard a hundred times. He noticed Willie's face in the mirror as he hung, the contorted grimace of bearing down to listen to the same old thing again. The noise of the motor would drown most of Sash out, at least for Willie. Spooky knew he was going to have to hear all of it.

"Well what happens is, Gilligan finds this old totem pole in the jungle and at the top is a carving that looks just like him...well, he chops it off because Professor tells him it's the dead koopakye king Bashooka, a god of the headhunters, and Gilligan wants no part of it because he thinks he's related and he doesn't want to have headhunter blood because he might go on a rampage and chop off everybody's head. Anyway, the headhunters find the chopped-off totem head and vow to kill the castaways... they capture the Howells and Ginger and Maryann and then tie them to poles until their head-shrinking water boils."

Spooky noticed the cans of 77 Marshall were spilled onto the street, and the trash bags had been torn open. "Looks like our raccoon is back," he said to Sash. They bent down and scooped up most of the debris, and flung it into the back, leaving a trail of chips and soggy noodles.

"To continue," Sash said. "Professor gets the idea to dress up Gilligan like the dead koopakye king Bashooka, so he might scare the headhunters into releasing the castaways. Him and Skipper try to teach Gilligan the koopakye words "pulu si bagoomba," which means "free the prisoners," so the headhunters would set the others free, but Gilligan can't get it right. Three simple words and he can't say 'free the prisoners' no matter how hard he tries. As he's practicing in front of a mirror screwing up the words, the headhunters capture the Skipper and Professor..."

Sash never finished telling the episode, about how Gilligan winds up saving them because he accidentally kicks the head after it falls off the totem pole and the headhunters think they chopped off the king's head and run away. Instead, Sash began calling out "pulu si bagoomba... pulu si bagoomba... pulu si bagoomba" as he picked up the cans, all the way up to the end of Marshall and then down Freemont and halfway across Sinkler. Free the prisoners, he was calling out to the sleeping masses long and loud. Free the prisoners.

Spooky lay with his thoughts after one fourteen-hour day, an exhausting affair in which he had to return with a truck from out past Midvale because the hydraulics had jammed on the compactor. By the time they took the replacement truck out, it was late afternoon and Sash was completely useless, asleep against the door and dreaming of Gilligan marathons, giving only a groaning response to Willie's kicks and yelling that he wanted to go home.

Spooky remembered back many summers, when the hydraulics had jammed on another truck. He had parked it at the end of the lot and it sat broken there that whole summer, because it would cost five grand to fix. So the company bought a new truck instead. He remembered walking across the lot one blistering afternoon and watching the old rusted truck as it swayed back and forth, as if a heavy wind was hitting against its side. He remembered thinking there must be someone rocking it from the other side because he couldn't figure what else could do something like that. "Them's maggots," Willie motioned. "Trapped in there all summer in this heat, hell, that truck is wall to wall maggots."

Spooky wanted to get out, to put his trash days behind him and start again somewhere, in something new and alive. He thought about bartending, or maybe an office job where he might learn all about computers and invoices and where he could wear fancy ties and put on cologne, and have a secretary who would open his mail and tell him what was important. Somebody would give him a company car with a moon-roof and he would smoke cigars dipped in Grand Marnier and watch the girls by a kidney pool beneath expensive sunglasses. Or maybe he would backpack through the Alps for a year with nothing but two pairs of jeans and a couple of golf shirts, a jelly sandwich and a road map. Or maybe he'd go back to school and learn some military history.

The images became murky as he drifted off, as he fell into a hot sleep, and for one defining moment he found himself nine years old and alone in his mother's living room back in Vermont, standing on the shiny hardwood floor in his pajamas, as the glare of the hall light stretched his shadow across the darkened room. Spooky stood before the pie table and looked up at his mother's expensive Hummel of a boy and his father fishing, plastered with permanent smiles. He stood just as he had stood thirty years ago, eyeing the thing and being frightened by it, because he was just some nine-year-old insignificant speck alongside it, especially after his mother's warning not to go near it because it was so expensive and not to touch anything else in the room, or the house for that matter. He remembered turning away, feeling the mighty intimidating impassivity of that figurine that reached out with invisible fingers and crushed his value to the level of dog shit, tugging away at his insides until he could no longer go near it.

In Spooky's dream the world was changed: he turned to the pie table and shoved it, then stood and watched the boy and his father go crashing to the floor, breaking into millions of pieces and spilling like water across the hardwood floor, little pieces of man and boy and smile. In this dream moment, the churning in his stomach had suddenly gone and he felt the invisible fingers let go of their hold. He felt alive and free as he stood over the million shards, as his shadow disappeared with the light coming through the picture window. Now he could do whatever he liked, free and alone. He was freefalling after that, like he'd done on the skydiving dare. As the silence enveloped him, he tried to stay suspended in the air in that dream spot, just float there with the wind pulling back his face, looking down forever at the muddy green fields. But he began to feel the tug of the earth pulling him down, pulling and then the muck of the swamp enveloping his ankles.

Spooky awoke and realized he needed to set the alarm. He wanted to get in early, because he had found out Willie just got a raise, and he wanted to ask Corky where was his pay-hike? He laid back down and thought about his alarm going off, that maybe he would be so tired this time that he would sleep right through the chirps, or that maybe the deafness creeping up on him would finally close his ears off for good. Drifting off, Spooky pictured 244 Worthington and the alarm that was going off there every morning he picked up their cans. He never remembered anything but the sound of that alarm, even above the grinding, it seemed. Coming out of the top room, that's all there ever was. Maybe it just went on and on and nobody ever bothered to shut it off.

MY SISTER SAID

JUST BEFORE I entered high school, my sister told me a series of horror stories concerning the making of *The Wizard of Oz*. One was that Margaret Hamilton, the actress who played the Wicked Witch, was secretly peddling, in her witch-of-the west-way, coffee to the public—and there were commercials to prove it. Maxwell House, my sister said, and the coffee is still very much around, so there you have it. She told me the Wicked Witch wanted a nation of caffeine addicts, and from what I saw with mom and dad, and at lunch counters wherever I went, the wicked witch was pretty much getting her way.

ANOTHER WAS THAT there were TWO TOTOS. *What happened to the first one?* was the natural first question. Well, as my sister tells it, it died on set. She was told by her best friend Grace that Billie Burke, the actress who played the Good Witch, often voiced her hatred of dogs, especially terriers, which she repeatedly called "yap dogs," and that Billie had yelled at least several times "get that nasty thing out of here" during filming. After Toto One's disappearance one afternoon, and as they were moving the cardboard trees for the next scene, Burke arrived late with a torn sleeve and with blood on the silver star of her magic wand. There were photographs with dark stains on the top tip of the star to prove it, her friend Grace said. Dead and bloodied behind the fake bushes, the terrier was discovered after a short search, and they quietly brought in a lookalike dog to finish the scenes after putting Toto One's carcass into a sack, my sister said.

BUT THE HORROR story from which I awoke from multiple nightmares was the story my sister told me of the hanging munchkin in the cardboard forest. You have to slow down the scene to see it, my sister said, and poof, the lifeless actor is there right on film, hanging by real rope from a thick cardboard branch that didn't break under the poor little man's weight. In my recurrent nightmares, the munchkin struggles to escape his noose, struggles to break his fake branch, because in my nightmare it wasn't suicide; someone had, my sister put into my ear, *hung him there* (Billie Burke? did she hate munchkins, too?) and he was struggling desperately to get free, all while the distracted crew helped fix the cowardly lion's mane. In my dream, munchkin legs flail, he gags, he squeals his last breath of life while the director Victor Fleming commands "take four!" And no one noticed the hanging munchkin until the fake forest was dismantled, my sister added, and no one even spotted the hanging munchkin on film until some *Wizard of Oz* nerd from the seventies slowed the film down and magnified the background trees. And that is the scary truth, my sister said. Go ahead and rent it and then push Pause!

Never mind my sister, though, and what she said. I am going to Paul's tomorrow and we're going to drop some acid and put on *The Wizard of Oz* and *Dark Side of the Moon* at the same time. We are going to partake in what he says is a "transformative experience" and "a disembarkation from reality." Paul said acid trips were like visiting another time and place, and you have to put yourself in a perfect situation to get to that time and place, and *Dark Side of the Moon*/*The Wizard of Oz* are the perfect ingredients. "They are tickets to the disembarkation," Paul said confidently.

I BELIEVE WHAT Paul says. High on acid, all things will be better, he promises, so never mind your fucking sister and what she says. Let me take you to a time and place where the coffee is not addictive, where terriers die peacefully, and where munchkins gather enough strength to escape nooses hanging from cardboard trees. All you need is some Pink Floyd.

TIM WENZELL teaches writing and literature courses at Virginia Union University in Richmond, Virginia. He is the author of the novel *Absent Children, Retrievals: Collected Poems, Emerald Green: An Ecocritical Study of Irish Literature*, and editor of *Woven Shades of Green: An Anthology of Irish Nature Literature*, as well as stories, poems, journalism, and ecocritical articles in many literary magazines and journals.